Fontamara

Fontamara
Ignazio Silone

Translated from the Italian by
Gwenda David and Eric Mosbacher

Fontamara: *Ignazio Silone*
April 1994
Redwords
31 Cottenham Road, Walthamstow, London E17 6RP

This edition of Fontamara published 1948

ISBN 1-872208-05-3

Design and production: Roger Huddle and Sofie Mason
Cover picture: detail from *The Fourth Estate* –
Giuseppe Pelizza da Volpedo (1868-1907)

Set in 10/12pt Adobe Goudy
Image setting by East End Offset
Printed by Cox & Wyman Ltd., Reading, Berkshire

Redwords would like to thank:
Eric Mosbacher
Gwenda David
David Shonfield
Mary Phillips
Clare Fermont
Mary Mason
Paul Foot
John Rees
Dot Pearce
for helping to publish this book

Fontamara

To
Romolo Tranquilli & Gabriella Seidenfeld

Foreword

The strange events I am about to describe took place in the course of a summer at Fontamara.

That was the name I gave to an old and obscure village in the Marsica, north of the reclaimed Lake Fucino in a valley halfway up between the hills and the mountains. Later I discovered that other places in southern Italy were already known by that name, sometimes with minor variations and, what was more serious, that strange things such as those that I faithfully record in this book also happened at a number of other places, though not at the same time or in the same sequence. But that did not seem to me to be a good reason for keeping quiet about them. There are plenty of names, such as Maria, Francesco, Giovanni, Lucia, Antonio and many others, that are common enough, and the really important things in life; birth, love, pain and death, are common to everyone, but people do not stop talking about them for that reason.

Well, then, in many ways Fontamara is just like every other rather remote southern Italian village between the plain and the mountains, away from the traffic arteries and therefore a little poorer and more abandoned and backward than the rest. But Fontamara also has characteristics of its own. Poor peasants, who make the soil productive and suffer from hunger – fellaheen, coolies, peons, mujiks, cafoni – are alike all over the world: they form a nation, a race, a church of their own, but two poor men identical in every respect have never yet been seen.

To anyone going up to Fontamara from the Fucino plain the village stands out against the grey, bleak, arid mountain-side as if it were on a flight of steps. The doors and windows of most of the houses are easily visible from below; there are about a hundred shapeless, irregular, hovels, nearly all of one floor only, blackened by time and worn by wind and rain and fire, with dilapidated roofs made up of tiles and scrap of all sorts.

Most of them have only a single opening that serves as door, window and chimney. They are generally unpaved and dry-walled and inside men, women and children, goats, chickens, pigs and donkeys live, sleep, eat and procreate their kind, sometimes in the same room. The exceptions are about a dozen houses belonging to small landowners and an old manor house, now empty and nearly falling to pieces. The upper part of Fontamara is dominated by a church with a bell-tower and a small, terraced square reached by a steep street that passes through the whole village and is the only one along which carts can pass. Narrow alleys lead off it, most of them short, steep and stepped, with roofs nearly touching one another and making it hardly possible to see the sky.

To anyone looking at it from a distance, from the Fucino estate, the village looks like a flock of dark sheep and the bell-tower looks like the shepherd. In short, it is a village like many others, but to those born and bred there it is the universe, for it is the scene of universal history – births, deaths, loves, hates, envies, struggles, and despair.

But for the strange events that I am about to describe there would be no more to say about Fontamara. I spent the

12

first twenty years of my life there, and that is all I should have to say about it.

For twenty years I knew the monotony of that sky, circumscribed by the amphitheatre of mountains that surround the estate like a barrier with no way out: for twenty years I knew the monotony of the earth, the rain, the wind, the snow, the saints' days, the food, the worries, the troubles and the poverty; the everlasting poverty, handed down by fathers who inherited it from grandfathers, in the face of which honest toil had never been of any use. The harshest injustices were of such long standing that they had acquired the naturalness of the rain, the wind and the snow. The life of men, of the beasts of the field and of the earth itself seemed enclosed in an immovable ring, held in the vice-like grip of the mountains and the changes of the season, welded into an unchanging natural cycle as in a kind of everlasting prison.

First came the sowing, then the spraying, then the reaping, then the gathering of the grapes. And then? The same thing over again. Sowing, hoeing, pruning, spraying, reaping, the gathering of the grapes. It was always the same song, always the same refrain. Years passed, years mounted up, the young grew old, the old died, and sowing, hoeing, spraying, reaping and gathering the grapes went on. And then? Back again to the beginning. Each year was like the previous year, each season like the one before, each generation like its predecessor. It has never occurred to anyone at Fontamara that this ancient way of life might change.

At Fontamara there are only two rungs on the social ladder: the lowest, that of the cafoni, which is at ground level, and that of the small landowners, which is just a little higher. The tradesmen are divided between the two; the less impoverished, who have a small shop or a few tools, are a little way up; the rest are at rock bottom. For generations the cafoni, the unskilled workers, the day labourers, the poor tradesmen, have suffered incredible privations and sacrifices trying to climb that lowest step of the social ladder, but only rarely have they succeeded. The height of good fortune is to marry a small landowner's daughter. But, if it is borne in mind that there is land around Fontamara where a man can sow a hundredweight of wheat and sometimes not harvest more than a hundredweight, it will be appreciated that it is not uncommon to relapse from the painfully acquired status of small landowner to that of cafone.

(I am well aware that in the current usage of my country cafone is a term of derision and contempt; but I use it in this book in the confident belief that when suffering ceases to be shameful in my country it will be a term of respect, and perhaps actually of honour.)

At Fontamara the better-off cafoni have a donkey, or sometimes even a mule. In the autumn, after struggling to pay off last year's debts, they have to borrow to buy the small amount of potatoes, beans, onions and maize flour necessary to avoid starving to death during the winter. Thus for most of them life consists of a heavy chain of small debts incurred to avoid starvation and the exhausting labour necessary to pay them off. When an exceptionally good harvest puts some unexpected cash into their pockets, it is generally spent on lawyers. Because at Fontamara there are no two families that are not related; in mountain villages everyone generally ends by being related to everyone else; every family, even the poorest, has interests that are shared with others, and for lack of wealth it is poverty that has to be shared; so at Fontamara there's not a family that does not have some case pending. In bad years litigation dies down, of course, but as soon as there's a little cash in hand to pay the lawyer it flares up again. The same never-ending cases are handed down interminably from generation to generation, involving never-ending expense and leaving in their wake an ineradicable trail of rancour and resentment, all to establish the ownership of a thicket of thorns. The thicket is burnt down, but the litigation continues more acrimoniously than ever.

There has never been any way out. Laying aside twenty

soldi a month, thirty soldi a month, in summer actually a hundred soldi a month might result in savings of about thirty lire by autumn. But they disappeared immediately; there would be interest that had to be paid off, or it would go to the lawyer or the priest or the chemist. Then next spring the same thing would begin all over again. Twenty soldi, thirty soldi, a hundred soldi a month. And then again back to the beginning.

Down on the plain many things changed, of course, at any rate in appearance, but nothing changed at Fontamara. The villagers watched the changes taking place below as if it were a play that had nothing to do with them. The mountain land they had to work was as barren and stony as ever, and there was as little of it as before, and the climate was still unfavourable. The reclamation of Lake Fucino that was carried out about eighty years ago benefited the communes on the plain but not those in the mountains, because it resulted in a marked reduction in temperature throughout the Marsica which actually ruined the traditional crops. The old olive groves were completely destroyed. The vineyards are often affected by disease and the grapes no longer fully ripen. They have to be hurriedly gathered at the end of October to avoid being frozen by the first snowfalls, and the wine that they yield is as sour as lemon juice. For the most part those who produce it are condemned to drink it.

Exploitation of the very fertile soil uncovered by the draining of the lake would have largely compensated for this havoc but for the fact that the Fucino basin was subjected to a colonial regime. The great wealth it yields annually enriches a privileged local minority while most of it migrates to the capital. For, in addition to a vast expanse of land in the Rome area and the Maremma, the 35,000 acres of the Fucino belong to the so-called princely family of Torlonia, who arrived in Rome at the beginning of the last century in the wake of a French regiment. But that is another story, and, to cheer the reader after this description of the sad fate of the people of Fontamara, one day perhaps I shall write an edifying life of the Torlogne family (Torlogne was their original name), which will certainly make much more entertaining reading. The obscure history of Fontamara is that of a monotonous calvary of land-hungry cafoni who for generation after generation have sweated blood from dawn to dusk to increase the size of a minute barren farm and have not succeeded in doing so, while the fate of the Torlognes was the precise opposite. None of them have ever worked the soil, even for pleasure, but their holdings have extended over thousands of acres.

They arrived in Rome in a time of war and speculated on the war. Then they speculated on the peace, and then on the salt monopoly, the troubles of 1848, the war of 1859, the Bourbons of the Kingdom of Naples and their downfall; later they speculated on the House of Savoy, then on the democratic régime and then on the dictatorship. Thus they gained thousands of millions of lire without taking off their gloves. After 1860 a Torlogne managed to pick up shares cheaply in a Neapolitan-Franco-Spanish finance company that had constructed the outlet for the draining of Lake Fucino but found itself in difficulties because of the collapse of the Neapolitan kingdom. The King of Naples had granted the company a ninety-year lease of the reclaimed land, but in return for Torlogne's political support of the weak Piedmontese dynasty this was extended to perpetuity and he was given the title of duke and later that of prince. In other words, the Piedmontese dynasty gave him something it did not possess. The Fontamaresi looked on at this performance down in the plain and, in spite of its novelty, they found it natural enough, since it was in harmony with traditional abuses of power. But in their mountains life continued as before.

There was a time when it was possible to escape to America. Before the war some Fontamaresi actually tried their luck in Argentina and Brazil. But those who managed to accumulate some bank notes between their vest and their shirt (on the side of the heart) and returned to Fontamara in a few years lost their small savings on the parched and barren soil of their native place and relapsed into the old lethargy, preserving like a vision of paradise lost the memory of a life glimpsed at beyond the sea.

But last year the life of Fontamara, which has been stagnant since time immemorial, was shaken to its foundations by a series of unexpected and incomprehensible events. No publicity was given to them at the time, and it was not till some months later that rumours began to trickle out to other parts of Italy and even abroad, where I, to my misfortune, have been forced to take refuge. Thus Fontamara, a place not even on the map, became the subject of strange conjectures and arguments. I was born and bred in the area and had been away for many years, but that did not prevent me from disbelieving these tales, from regarding the things that were alleged to have happened at Fontamara as imaginary and utterly fantastic, invented out of thin air for questionable motives, like so many other stories, and attributed to that remote spot because that made them more difficult to check. Some attempts I made to get direct news failed. Yet not a single day passed on which I did not return in my imagination to that place that I knew so well, and did not think about it and long to know what had happened to it. And then a strange thing happened. One evening, when I was feeling particularly homesick, to my great surprise I found three cafoni, two men and a woman, sitting outside my front door, leaning against it and almost asleep. I recognised them at once as coming from Fontamara. They rose and followed me into the house. I recognised their faces by the light of the lamp. One was a tall, thin old man with a grey, stubbly face; the others were his wife and son. They came in, sat down, and began to talk. Then I recognised their voices too.

The old man spoke first. Then his wife took up the tale, then the man again and then his wife, and while she was

17

talking I fell asleep – and this was a most extraordinary phenomenon – without losing the thread of what she was saying:
as if her voice came from the deepest depths inside me.
When dawn broke and I awoke the man was talking again.

What they said is in this book.

But first two points must be made clear. To the foreign
reader, who will be the first to read it, this tale will be in
striking contrast to the picturesque vision of southern Italy
often conjured up in tourist literature. In some books, of
course, southern Italy is a blessed and beautiful land in
which the peasants go carolling joyfully to work, echoed
prettily by a chorus of country girls in traditional costume,
while nightingales trill in the neighbouring wood.

But no such marvel has ever happened at Fontamara.

Its people – dress like the poor do all over the world.
There is no wood at Fontamara. The mountainside is
parched and bare-like the greater part of the Apennines, in
fact. The birds are few and timid, because of the pitiless way
in which they are hunted, and there are certainly no
nightingales. There is not even a word for nightingale in the
local dialect. The peasants do not sing, either in chorus or
alone. They do not sing even when drunk, let alone on their
way to work. They do not sing, they swear. They swear to
express any strong feeling, whether joy or anger, or even religious devotion. There is not much imagination even in their
swearing. They merely swear by the two or three saints they
know, always using the same crude oaths.

In my youth the only person who used to sing in
Fontamara was a cobbler, and he knew only one song, and
that dated back to the beginning of our first war in Africa
and began like this:

Oh, Baldissera,

Beware of the blacks . . .

The repetition of this piece of advice every day of the
year, from morning to night, delivered in a voice that
became more and more lugubrious as the cobbler grew older,

in the course of time gave rise to a widespread fear among the young people of Fontamara that General Baldissera, whether from foolhardiness, absence of mind or sheer negligence, might perhaps end by trusting the blacks after all. Many years later we learned that this had actually happened before we were born, with catastrophic results.

The second point is this. In what language ought I to tell this story?

Do not imagine for one moment that the inhabitants of Fontamara talk Italian. To us Italian is a language learnt at school, like Latin, French or Esperanto. To us it is a foreign language, a dead language, a language the vocabulary and grammar of which developed without any connection with us or our way of behaving or thinking or expressing ourselves.

Of course other southern cafoni before me have spoken Italian and written it, just as when we go to town we wear shoes and collars and ties. But one glance at us is sufficient to reveal our discomfort. The Italian language cripples and deforms our thoughts, and cannot help giving them the flavour of a translation. But to express himself a man should not have to translate. If it is true that to be able to express yourself well in school Italian you have first to learn to think in it, the effort that it costs us to talk that kind of Italian obviously means that we can't think in it. In other words, to us that kind of Italian culture is still school culture.

But, since I have no other way of communicating what I have to say (and expressing myself is now an absolute necessity to me) I shall make the best job I can of translating, into the language that we learnt at school, what I want everyone to know, the truth about what happened at Fontamara.

Even though we tell the story in a borrowed tongue, the way of telling it will, I think, be our own. That at least is one of the arts of Fontamara. We learnt it when we were children, sitting on the doorstep, or round the fireplace in the long nights of winter, or by the hand loom, listening to the old stories to the rhythm of the pedal.

The art of story-telling, the art of putting one word after another, one line after another, one sentence after another, explaining one thing at a time, without allusions or reservation, calling bread bread and wine wine, is just like the ancient art of weaving, the ancient art of putting one thread after another, one colour after another, cleanly, neatly, perseveringly, plainly for all to see. First you see the stem of the rose, then the calyx, then the petals. You can see from the beginning that it is going to be a rose, and for that reason townsfolk think our products coarse and crude. But have we ever gone to town and tried to sell them? Have we ever asked townspeople to tell their story in our fashion? No, we have not.

Let everyone, then, have the right to tell his story in his own way.

Ignazio Silone
Davos, Summer 1930

1   On the first of June last year Fontamara went
without electric light for the first time. Fontamara remained
without electric light on the second, the third and the fourth
of June.

So it continued for days and months. In the end
Fontamara got used to moonlight again. A century had
elapsed between the moonlight era and the electric era, a
century which included the age of oil and that of petrol, but
one evening was sufficient to plunge us back from electric
light to the light of the moon.

Young people don't know the story, but we old folks
know it. All the innovations the Piedmontese brought us
Southern peasants in the space of seventy years boil down to
two: electric light and cigarettes. They took the electric light
away again, and as for the cigarettes, those who've smoked
them may choke for all we care. Tobacco has always been
good enough for us.

It shouldn't have been a surprise to us the first time the
electric light was cut off, but it was a surprise all the same.

Electric light had come to be accepted as practically a
natural phenomenon, in the sense that nobody at Fontamara
ever paid for it. Nobody had paid for it for many months. As
a matter of fact, the district collector hadn't even come
round delivering the monthly bills and warning notices for
those who were in arrears. We used the bits of paper he distributed as pipe-cleaners. The last time he came round he
only just managed to get away with a whole skin. He was
lucky not to be laid out by a bullet at the parish boundary.

The man certainly thought discretion the better part of
valour. He would come to Fontamara when the men were at

work and only women and children were at home. He was exceedingly polite. He would deliver his pieces of paper with an idiotic, conciliatory grin.

'Take one,' he would say, 'it won't do you any harm; a bit of paper always comes in handy about the house. '

But politeness wasn't enough. One day – not in Fontamara, for he pretty soon gave up setting foot in the place, but down below in our local town – a carter gave him a pretty plain hint that if a shot was fired it wouldn't so much be aimed at him, Innocenzo La Legge, personally, as at the taxes in general. But if a shot had hit its mark it wouldn't have been the taxes that would have been done away with, but he, Innocenzo La Legge. So he didn't come any more, and nobody missed him. The idea of starting legal proceedings against the inhabitants of Fontamara he did not consider a practical one.

'There's no doubt that legal proceedings would be highly effective if it were possible to seize lice,' he said once. 'But as there's no legal means of doing that the only thing to do is to cut off the electric light.'

The light was to have been cut off on the first of January. Then it was to have been the first of March, then the first of May, then the first of June. Finally on the first of June it was cut off.

The women and children who were at home were the last to notice it. But we men on our way home from work did notice it. Some of us had been at the mill and were coming home by the main road; some had been up at the cemetery and were coming home down the mountain-side; some had been at the sandpit and were coming home along the stream; and the others, who had been out day-labouring, were coming home from all directions. As it gradually got darker and we saw the lights of the neighbouring villages being turned on and Fontamara still in darkness, getting lost so that you couldn't make it out among the trees and the thickets and the dungheaps – all of a sudden it dawned on us what it really was. It was a surprise and yet it wasn't.

The children thought it a tremendous joke. Our children don't often have anything to joke about, so when they do get a chance they take it – the passing of a motor-cyclist, the coupling of two donkeys or a chimney on fire, for instance.

When we got back we found poor General Baldissera in despair. During the summer he used to mend boots until late at night by the light of the street-lamp in front of his house. A crowd of children had surrounded his table, upset his nails and knives and priser, his wax and hemp and scraps of leather, and turned his bucket of filthy water over his feet. He was cursing at the top of his voice by all the saints of the neighbourhood, and he wanted to know what he'd done at his age, half blind as he was, that he should be deprived of the light of the street-lamp; and what would King Humbert have thought of such an outrage?

It was difficult to imagine what King Humbert would have thought of it.

Of course a lot of women were there, complaining bitterly. There's no point in mentioning names. They were sitting on the ground in front of their houses or feeding their babies or busy with the cooking, and some of them were lamenting as if somebody had just died. They wept over the cutting off of the electric light as though their wretchedness were made more pitiful by the dark.

Michele Zompa and I stopped at the table in front of Marietta Sorcanera's bar, and Giacobbe Losurdo turned up with the she-ass he'd taken to stud, and soon after Ponzio Pilato turned up with the sulphur-pump on his back, and then Antonio Ranocchia and Baldovino Sciarappa, who had been pruning, and Giacinto Barletta, Venerdì Santo, Ciro Zironda, Papasisto and others who had been to the sand-pit. We all started talking at once about the electric light and about the taxes – the new taxes, the old taxes, the district taxes, the State taxes – repeating the same old things we'd said hundreds of times before, because these things don't alter. Suddenly we noticed that a stranger was among us, a stranger with a bicycle. It was difficult to guess who it might be at that time of day.

He wasn't the electric-light man, and he wasn't the district officer either; nor was he the man from the police office. He was a very smart young man indeed, with an exquisite, well-shaven face, and a tiny little pink mouth. The hand with which he was holding the handle-bars of his bicycle was small and sticky, like the under-side of a lizard. He wore white spats.

We stopped talking. It was obvious that the little fellow had come to announce a new tax. There could be no possible doubt about it whatever. Nor could there be any doubt that he was completely wasting his time and that his pieces of paper would share the fate of those of Innocenzo La Legge. The only thing in doubt was: what on earth was there left on which a new tax could be put? We all racked our brains but nobody could think of anything.

Meanwhile the stranger, in a silly, nanny-goat's voice, had already asked two or three times if someone could show him the way to the house of the widow of the heroic Sorcanera.

The widow of the heroic Sorcanera was there, at the bar door, obstructing the entrance with her grotesque, pregnant form – it was her third or fourth pregnancy since the death of her husband in the war. Her husband had left her a silver medal and a pension, but he hadn't left her the three or four pregnancies. Her husband having died a hero, Sorcanera had subsequently had frequent dealings with persons of consequence. Once, at a solemn patriotic ceremony in the local town, Sorcanera had been given a seat at the high table, next to the bishop. Her pregnancies always assumed obscene, monstrous shapes. The bishop wasn't blind.

'So you have married again, my good lady,' he said to her. She answered that she had not. The bishop, in some surprise, made some allusion to her undeniable pregnancy, and

Marietta, taken unawares, answered: 'It is a legacy from my late husband. . .'

It is evident, therefore, that Sorcanera knew how to deal with persons of consequence. She offered the stranger a seat at the table. He took a large bundle of papers from his pocket and laid them on the table.

When we saw the papers we had, if possible, less doubt about it than ever. They were the papers dealing with the tax. The question still remained: what tax could it be?

The stranger began to speak. We knew at once that he was a man from town. We managed to understand a few words here and there, but we couldn't grasp what tax he was talking about.

Meanwhile it was getting late. There we were, with our tools – our hoes and pickaxes and forks and shovels and the sulphur-pump and Giacobbe Losurdo's donkey. Some of us went away. Venerdì Santo, Giacinto Barletta and Papasisto went away. Baldovino Sciarappa and Antonio Ranocchia listened to the gibberish a little longer and then went away too. Giacobbe Losurdo wanted to stay, but the donkey, who was tired, persuaded him to go home as well.

There were three of us left, besides the man from town.

He went on talking, but nobody understood a word. I mean no one grasped what it was on which another tax had been put, or what there was on which another tax could be put.

In the end the man stopped talking. He turned to me – I was nearest him – and held out a pencil and a blank sheet of paper and said:

'Sign, please.'

What did he want us to sign for? We hadn't understood ten words of his whole speech, but even if we had, what on earth was there to sign for?

He turned to the man next to me, held out the pencil and the piece of paper and said once more:

'Sign, please.'

The man next to me didn't answer either. The man from town turned to the third man, held out the pencil and piece of paper again and said:

'You sign first. If you sign the others will sign too.'

He might have been talking to a brick wall. Nobody breathed a word. We hadn't the slightest idea what it was all about, so why on earth should we sign?

The man from town got positively angry. From his tone of voice we thought he must be insulting us. But he didn't say anything about taxes. We were waiting for him to begin talking about some new tax, but he would go on talking about other things. At one point he took a riding-whip which was tied to the bicycle-frame and began brandishing it in my face.

'Talk, can't you, damn you?' he shrieked. 'Why can't you answer when you're spoken to? Why won't you sign?' I explained to him that we weren't idiots, that we couldn't make out what he was driving at and that, in spite of all his talk, we were quite certain it was a new tax he had come about.

'We know all about it already,' I told him. 'We know only too much about it. But we shan't pay. There's a house tax, and a vineyard tax, and a donkey tax, and a dog tax, and a pasture tax, and a pig tax, and a wagon tax, and a wine tax, and that's about enough. What is it you want to put another tax on?'

The man looked at me as if I had been talking Hebrew. He seemed a little discouraged.

'We've been talking and not understanding each other,' he said. 'We talk the same language, and yet we don't talk the same language.'

That was true enough. A man from town and a peasant cannot possibly understand each other. He talked like a man from town, he couldn't help talking like a man from town, he couldn't talk any other way. And we were peasants. We understood everything as peasants, that is, in our own way. I have noticed thousands of times during my life that people from town and peasants are entirely different. In my youth I was in the Argentine, on the pampas. I talked to peasants of all races, from Spaniards to Indians, and we understood one another as if we were at Fontamara. Every Sunday I used to talk to an Italian who came from a town – he was from the consulate. We used to talk without understanding each other; sometimes we actually understood the opposite of what was meant.

So I wasn't in the least surprised when the stranger started his gibberish all over again and explained to us that he wasn't talking to us about taxes, that he had nothing whatever to do with taxes and that he had come to Fontamara for a different reason altogether and that there was nothing to pay.

As it was late and had got dark by this time he started lighting matches. He showed us the sheets of paper, one by one. They really were blank sheets and not tax demands. They were perfectly blank. Something was written at the top of one sheet only. The man lit two matches and showed us what it was.

'The undersigned of their own free will and volition have given their signatures to the Hon. Pelino, Commander of Militia, in enthusiastic support of what is stated above.'

The man explained that he was the Hon. Pelino, and that the sheets, when duly signed, would be sent to the Government.

The Hon. Pelino had been given the sheets of paper by his superiors. Identical sheets of paper had been taken to other villages by colleagues of his. They were not specially for Fontamara, they were for all the villages. They constituted, in fact, a petition to the Government, a petition for which many signatures were necessary. It was true that he hadn't got the petition with him and that he did not know what was in it. It would be written by his superiors. All he had to do was to collect the signatures, and all the peasants had to do was to sign it.

'The time when the country folk were ignored and despised has gone for ever,' he explained. 'There are new authorities in office now, who hold the peasants in high esteem and wish to give consideration to their views. So I appeal to you to give me your signatures. Show your appreciation of the honour that the authorities have done you in sending an official here to consult your wishes.'

We were still a little suspicious, but meanwhile General Baldissera had turned up and he had heard the last few words of the official's explanations. 'Very well,' he said, with no more ado (you know what these cobblers are). 'If the honourable gentleman assures me that there's nothing to pay, I'll sign first.'

He did sign first. Then I signed, and then Ponzio Pilato, who was next to me, and then Michele Zompa and then Marietta. But what about the others? How could signatures be obtained at that time of night? At that hour it was impossible to go from door to door collecting them. The Hon. Pelino had an idea. We should dictate to him the names of all the peasants of Fontamara and he would register them. And so we did. There was a lively argument in one case only, that of Berardo Viola. We tried to explain to the Hon. Pelino that Berardo wouldn't have signed on any account, but his name was put down too.

The second sheet was already filled up with names and the stranger had already lit thirty or forty matches when he noticed something on the table. It seemed to fascinate and horrify him. But there wasn't anything there. He lit a match and examined the table carefully. He bent over it and nearly touched it with his nose. Then, pointing a finger at the table, he began to shriek at the top of his nanny-goat's voice:

'What is this? To whom does this filthy thing belong? Who dared put it on the table?'

It was obvious that he was looking for trouble. nobody answered. General Baldissera prudently went home. The stranger repeated his question four or five times, and lit three matches at once to make a better light. Then we did see something on the table – something moving.

Ponzio Pilato got up first, bent over the table, looked at it carefully, and said:

'It's not mine!'

I did the same. I looked at it, touched it, turned it round and round with the stem of my pipe. Really it wasn't mine, on my word of honour. Michele Zompa pretended not to have understood and went on smoking, looking into space. Marietta bent over the table too, took a prolonged look at the insect, which by this time had reached the middle of the sheet of paper covered with names, took it in the palm of her hand and threw it into the middle of the street.

'What an extraordinary thing,' she said. 'Quite extraordinary. A new kind of louse – long, dark coloured, and with a cross on its back!'

Michele Zompa jumped to his feet and began to shout:

'What! What! Did it really have a cross on its back? And you've thrown it away? Do you mean to say you've actually thrown away the Pope's own louse? The louse of the Conciliation? You ought to be excommunicated, you wretched, sacrilegious woman, you!'

None of us understood what this outburst was all about, so Michele explained.

'It's a dream I dreamt last winter,' he said. 'I told it to Don Abbacchio, and he ordered me not to tell anybody. But now IT has appeared, if what Marietta says is true, and as IT has appeared I can tell you. This is what it was all about:

'You remember that after peace was made between the Pope and the Government, Don Abbacchio explained to us from the altar steps that a good time was coming for the peasants. The Pope obtained a grace from Christ to give the peasants whatever they needed. I saw the Pope talking with Jesus in my dream.

'Jesus said: "In order to celebrate the conclusion of this

peace it would be as well to distribute the land of the Fucino among the peasants who cultivate it."

'The Pope replied: "O Lord, the Prince Torlonia would not agree to that . . . Do not forget that Prince Torlonia makes a handsome contribution to St. Peter's Purse."

'Jesus said: "In order to celebrate the conclusion of this peace it would be well to dispense the peasants from the payment of taxes."

'The Pope replied: "O Lord, the Government would not agree to that. Do not forget that it is with the aid of the taxes the peasants pay that the Government is able to pay two thousand million lire to St. Peter's Purse."

'Jesus said: "In order to celebrate this peace it would be well to grant an abundant harvest, above all to the peasants and the small landowners."

'The Pope replied: "O Lord, if the peasants' crops are abundant the prices of agricultural produce will fall. Do not forget that our bishops and cardinals are all large landowners."

'Jesus was grieved at not being able to do anything for the peasants without doing harm to somebody else. And so the Pope, who loves the peasants dearly, said:

' "O Lord, let us go and see for ourselves. Perhaps it may be possible after all to do something for the peasants which will displease neither Prince Torlonia nor the Government nor the bishops nor the cardinals."

'So on the night of the Conciliation Christ and the Pope came flying over the Fucino and all the villages of the Marsica. Christ went in front, with a large bag on His shoulders, and behind Him came the Pope, who had permission to take from it whatever might be useful to the peasants.

'In every village the Holy Visitors saw the same thing. The peasants were grumbling, cursing, squabbling and growing poorer, not knowing which way to look for food or clothes. And the Pope was afflicted in his heart at what he saw. So he took from the bag a whole cloud of lice and released them over the Marsica, saying:

' "Take them, my beloved children, and scratch your-selves. Thus in your moments of leisure you will have some-thing to distract your thoughts from sin!" '

That was Michele Zompa's dream. Everyone interprets dreams his own way, of course, and lots of people don't take them seriously at all. Many use them to foretell the future. All I think them good for is to send you to sleep. But Marietta Sorcanera, who is very religious, thought otherwise. Anyway, she burst out crying most pitifully and said, between her sobs:

'It's perfectly true, it's perfectly true! Who would there be to keep us from sin if there were no Pope to pray for us? Who would there be to save us from damnation?'

The Hon. Pelino, however, interpreted all this quite dif-ferently.

'You're making a laughing-stock of me,' he shouted, bran-dishing his riding-whip at Zompa and Sorcanera. 'You're making a laughing-stock of me. You're mocking at the authorities. You're mocking at the Government and at the Church.'

And so on in the same strain. We didn't in the least fol-low what he was driving at.

'The Government will put you in your places,' he said. 'The Government will punish you. You'll hear more about this from the authorities.'

He'll go on talking, but in the end he'll shut up, we thought to ourselves. He went on, however. He wouldn't shut up.

'Don't you know that if I denounced you you'd be sen-tenced to at least ten years' imprisonment?' he shouted at Michele. 'Don't you know that there are many doing ten years' hard labour for saying things far less harmful and sedi-tious than what you've just said? What world are you living in, man? Do you or do you not know what has been happen-ing in the last few years? Don't you know who's the master now? Don't you know who's in command?'

Zompa answered him patiently, to calm him down.

'Look here,' he said. 'In town lots of things happen. In town at least one thing happens every day. Every day a news-paper comes out and reports at least one happening. How many happenings does that make at the end of the year? Hundreds and hundreds. How on earth can a poor worm of a peasant know everything that's happened? It's impossible. But things that happen are one thing, the people in com-mand are quite another. The people in command are the authorities. Sometimes they change their names, but they're always the authorities.'

'And the hierarchy? What about the hierarchy?' asked the townsman, who was probably a hierarch himself. You see, we didn't yet know what the word meant. The man had to repeat it over and over again, and explain it in different terms. In the end Michele answered:

'At the head of everything is God, Lord of Heaven.

'After Him comes Prince Torlonia, lord of the earth.

'Then come Prince Torlonia's armed guards.

'Then come Prince Torlonia's armed guards' dogs.

'Then, nothing at all. Then nothing at all. Then nothing at all. Then come the peasants. And that's all.'

'And the authorities, where do they come in?' asked the man from town, more angrily than ever.

Ponzio Pilato interrupted to explain that the authorities were divided between the third and fourth categories, according to the pay. The fourth category (that of the dogs) was a very large one.

The Hon. Pelino rose to his feet. He was quivering with rage. He said: 'I promise you you'll hear more of this.' And away he went.

2   Next day at dawn an extraordinary thing happened and the whole of Fontamara was in an uproar.

A poor, thin spring rises from beneath a heap of stones at the entrance to Fontamara and forms a dirty pool. A few paces away the water burrows into the stony soil and disappears, to reappear later in the form of a more abundant stream at the bottom of the hill. The stream makes a number of bends and then flows in the direction of the Fucino. The peasants of Fontamara have always drawn their water from it, to water the few fields they possess down in the valley, which form their only wealth. Furious quarrels about sharing out the water break out every summer. In years of drought these quarrels end in stabbing affrays.

The first Fontamara peasants to go down the hill on the second of June on their way to work met a group of roadmenders who had come from the local town with picks and shovels (or so they told us) to divert the stream from its course between the fields and gardens it had always watered, ever since earth and water began, and re-direct it so as to border some vineyards, and water some land that did not belong to Fontamara at all. It belonged to a wealthy landowner from the local town, called Don Carlo Magna, because at whatever time of day anybody called on him and asked: 'Is Don Carlo at home?' the maid would always answer: 'Don Carlo? *magna*, he's at table, but you can see madam if you like.'

For a moment or two we thought the road-menders were playing a practical joke on us, for playing practical jokes on us was a favourite pastime of the people from the local town. A whole day wouldn't be enough to describe all the jokes they had played on us in the last few years. The story of the donkey and the priest will give some idea of the kind of thing they did.

There never has been a priest at Fontamara. The revenue from the church is not sufficient to support one. So the church was only open on high days and holy days, when Don Abbacchio used to come from the local town to say Mass and preach the Gospel.

Two years ago the people of Fontamara sent a special appeal to the bishop to send us a parish priest. A few days later we learnt that our prayer had been answered and that we were to prepare to celebrate the arrival of our first parish priest. Naturally we did our best to give him a fine reception. The church was given a thorough good cleaning. The road leading to Fontamara was mended and in some places actually widened. A big triumphal arch was built at the entrance to Fontamara. The doors of all the houses were decorated with green branches. When the great day arrived the whole village turned out to meet the new priest. After walking for a quarter of an hour we saw a large crowd of people coming towards us. We went on to meet them, singing hymns and reciting the Rosary. In front walked the elders, among them General Baldissera, who was to make a short speech, and the women and children brought up the rear. When we'd got quite near to the people from the town we divided into two ranks along either side of the road to welcome our priest.

General Baldissera went on by himself, shouting:

'Blessed be Jesus! Blessed be the Virgin Mary! Blessed be the Church!'

At that moment the crowd of townspeople divided too, and the new priest, in the shape of an old donkey adorned with sacred ornaments, advanced towards us, urged on by kicks and stones.

Jokes of that kind were not easily forgotten, even if the townspeople constantly invented new ones. So we naturally concluded the diversion of the stream was a practical joke, too. After all, it would be the end of everything if men started interfering with the elements created by God, and diverted the course of the sun, the course of the winds, and the course of the waters established by God. It would be like hearing that donkeys were learning to fly, or that Prince Torlonia was no longer a prince or that the peasants were no longer hungry; in other words, that the laws of God were no longer the laws of God.

But the road-menders, without any explanation whatever, had put their hands to their picks and shovels to dig the new stream-bed. That seemed carrying the joke a little too far. A peasant rushed back to Fontamara to give the alarm.

'Run, quick! Warn the police! Warn the mayor!' he shouted.

The men couldn't go. In June there's far too much work in the fields. So the women had to go. My wife will tell you what happened next.

Well, you know what women are like. This is what happened. The sun was already high before we even started.

At first nobody could go. One had to look after her chickens, another after her pigs. Another couldn't go because it was washing-day. Another had to prepare the mixture for spraying the vines, another had to get sacks ready for threshing, another had to go and cut grass for the goats. At first, in fact, nobody could go at all. Only Sorcanera volunteered, because she knew how to talk to the authorities, or so she said.

She found another woman to go with her. There's no need to mention her name, for she was pregnant, too. Her husband had been in America for ten years, and it was difficult to believe that he had achieved this result from such a distance.

'Can we allow Fontamara, in a matter that affects every single one of us, to be represented by two women who are, speaking with all due respect, two whores?' I said to Zompa's wife.

We certainly could not. So we went to Lisabetta Limona and Maria Grazia and persuaded them to come, too. Maria Grazia brought along Ciammaruga, and she brought along Cannarozzo's daughter, who in turn brought Filomena Quaterna.

We were all ready to start when Ponzio Pilato's wife started making a fuss because we hadn't asked her.

'You want to go behind our backs, do you?' she screamed. 'You want to put yourself forward at the expense of all the rest, do you? Do you suppose my husband's land doesn't need water any more?'

So we had to wait while she got dressed. But instead of dressing she went and fetched Filomena Castagna, Recchiuta, Giuditta Scarpone and Fornara, and persuaded them to come along, too. In the end there were at least fifteen of us waiting outside Baldissera's shop, ready to start. We had to wait a bit longer because Sorcanera was still dressing. At last she turned up in her Sunday best, with a new apron, coral beads round her neck and the hero's silver medal on her bosom.

'A nice new apron on a nice new belly,' said Baldissera, grinning. He pretended to be shortsighted but he could see plainly enough when he chose. Marietta grinned herself.

The sun was high in the heavens when at last we started. The heat was stifling.

When the road-menders saw us they were terrified and ran away towards the vineyards.

When Lisabetta Limona saw this she decided that we had obtained the desired effect and wanted to turn back, but Sorcanera, in her new apron, said we ought to go on all the same, because, after all, the men were not acting on their own initiative but only carrying out orders. We started arguing about what to do next, but Marietta cut it short.

'If you're frightened, we'll go on alone,' she said, meaning herself and the other woman who was pregnant by the Holy Ghost; and the two of them went on towards the local town.

'We cannot possibly allow Fontamara to be represented by two women who are, speaking with all due respect, two whores,' we said to one another, and on we all went behind Sorcanera.

It was midday when we got to town. Our arrival in the town hall square caused quite a panic. Certainly our appearance was not very reassuring. The shopkeepers ran out of their shops and put up their shutters. A number of fruit-sellers who were standing in the middle of the square rushed away with their baskets on their heads. People swarmed to all the windows and balconies. A few terrified clerks appeared at the town hall door. Everybody seemed to be expecting us to take the town hall by storm. We advanced grimly, ready for anything.

At that moment a rural guard put his head out of the window and started shouting:

'Don't let them in! They'll fill the whole place with lice!'

The crowd burst out laughing.

They all burst out laughing, those who a moment before had been frightened out of their wits and had started running away, and those who a moment before had shut their shops or fled with their baskets on their heads. They all laughed. We huddled together against the door of the town hall. The rural guard, success going to his head, started telling incredible stories about us and our lice. Everybody in the square roared with laughter. A lady on a balcony facing us laughed so much that she held her sides. A watchmaker, taking down the shutters of his shop, laughed so much that he almost cried. More clerks and typists had collected at the town hall door, and they were all laughing noisily, too.

We had no idea what to do next. On the way Sorcanera had told us to leave it all to her, but she was at a loss when confronted by all those laughing people. If it had been the rural guard alone, it would have been easy to answer him back, because in his youth it hadn't been only on others that he had seen lice crawl. But there were all those other people to deal with.

A clerk asked us: 'Whom do you want to see? What is it you want?'

'We want to talk to his worship the mayor,' said Marietta.

The clerks at the gate looked at each other in astonishment. Some of them repeated the question:

'Whom do you want?'

'We want to see the mayor,' four or five of us answered, all speaking at the same time.

The clerks all started laughing again like maniacs. They repeated our demand at the top of their voices, and everybody in the square, at the windows, on the verandas, and in the neighbouring dining-rooms (it was lunch-time by now) burst out laughing again.

Then, as it was midday, all the clerks came out of the town hall and one of them shut the gates.

'Do you really want to talk to the mayor?' he said to us as he was leaving. 'Wait here, then. You may have to wait for some time.'

It was not till afterwards that we understood what he was driving at. In the meantime our attention was attracted by a drinking-fountain we saw in a corner of the square. We all dashed towards it. A real cat-and-dog fight broke out. We were all thirsty, but we couldn't all drink at once. Marietta's claim to drink first because of her pregnancy was not admitted. After a good deal of pushing and shoving we settled the order in which to drink. Giuditta Scarpone drank first, and then a girl with a sore on her lip. We wanted her to drink last, but she seized hold of the tap and wouldn't let go. Marietta's turn came next, but just as she was going to drink the water gave out.

It might have been just a momentary stoppage, so we waited. But the water didn't come back. The fountain was dead. We were just going away when we heard the water coming again, so we turned back. Another scrap started, and more squabbling. Two girls started tearing each other's hair.

We settled the order in which we were going to drink all over again, but the water suddenly failed once more. We waited a little, but it didn't come back.

The behaviour of the water was absolutely baffling. Nothing like it had ever happened to the spring at the entrance to Fontamara. The watchmaker and the rural guard were watching us from the other side of the square, laughing.

It may seem stupid to waste time telling you all this when far, far worse things happened later on. But I simply couldn't get out of my head this extraordinary business of the water which disappeared before our thirst. This is what happened each time. As the water didn't come back, we went away from the fountain, but as soon as we moved away it came back. And that happened three or four times. As soon as we went back the water stopped immediately and the fountain dried up. As soon as we moved away again the water promptly returned. We were parched with thirst and it was impossibly to drink. As soon as we got near the water it vanished.

After this had happened for the fourth time a dozen gendarmes came up to us, surrounded us, and asked us what we wanted.

'We want to talk to the mayor,' we said.

'The mayor? The mayor?' the sergeant exclaimed. 'Don't you know that there aren't any mayors now? When will you get it into your heads that the mayor is now called the *podestà?*"

Whatever he was called, it was all the same to us. But it was obviously a matter of vast importance to educated people, otherwise the clerks wouldn't have laughed so much at our asking to see the mayor and not the *podestà*, and the sergeant wouldn't have got so angry. But educated people are fussy and lose their tempers over very little.

The sergeant ordered four gendarmes to accompany us to the *podestà*. Two gendarmes led the way and two brought up the rear. Passers-by shouted and jeered at us. People in large towns, especially workmen and apprentices, have always taken pleasure in ridiculing peasants from the villages.

The gendarmes took us down the main street and then down a lot of streets we didn't know. We passed the house of the old mayor, Don Circostanza, but, to our great surprise, the gendarmes didn't stop. We were very surprised indeed to discover that Don Circostanza was no longer mayor. We expected to be taken next to Don Carlo Magna's house, but the gendarmes led us straight by without stopping there either. On we went, and soon we were out of the town among the fields again.

'The gendarmes are fooling us,' we said to one another. 'The mayor can't possibly be anybody but Don Circostanza. He was mayor before the War and during the War and after the War; and during the brief spells that he wasn't mayor Don Carlo Magna was. Since the gendarmes have passed both their houses without stopping they are obviously going to play some dirty trick on us.'

The gendarmes led us along a path encumbered with building materials – bricks, lime, sand, girders and iron sheets – and it was difficult enough for us to get along it at all. But at last we got to the gate of a newly built villa that belonged to a Roman known at Fontamara as the Contractor. The villa was decorated with flags and little coloured paper lamps. Several women were beating and brushing carpets in the courtyard. The gendarmes stopped right in front of the villa gate.

'What! Has that brigand been made mayor? An outsider like him! It's impossible!' Not one of us could help expressing our amazement.

'He was appointed yesterday,' the gendarmes told us. 'The telegram appointing him *podestà* arrived from Rome yesterday.'

Three years ago, when the Contractor first arrived from Rome, nobody knew who he was or where he was born. He took lodgings at an inn and started buying up apples in the month of May, when the apples were still on the trees and the peasants needed the money. Then he started buying up onions, beans, lentils, tomatoes. Everything he bought he sent to Rome. Then he started breeding pigs and, later, horses. In the end he had a finger in every pie; he dealt in rabbits, honey, skins, land, brickworks, timber. He engaged in road-making. You saw him at every fair and every market throughout the district. At first the old landowners looked down on him and refused to have any truck with him, but one by one he got the better of them all. There wasn't a single important deal in which he didn't manage to outdo them. In the end they got suspicious and actually denounced him as a forger. Official inquiries revealed the existence of a banknote factory which provided the money for all his enterprises, but the banknotes were legal, because the factory belonged to a bank.

There was a lot of discussion at Fontamara about this strange fact, which no one was willing to admit. We knew from our own experience and from all we'd ever heard that you can use a bank for safeguarding your money, or sending it from America to Italy, or for changing it into the money of another country. But what on earth had a bank to do with business? How could a bank be interested in pig-breeding or house-building or tanneries or brickworks?

After the inquiry the Contractor's authority increased enormously. He represented the bank. He had a mint at his disposal. The old landowners began to tremble before him. All the same we couldn't quite understand why they had ever let him be made mayor.

The women at work in the courtyard fetched Rosalia, the Contractor's wife, as soon as they saw us. She came out raging like a fury. She was getting on in years and was all dressed up like a townswoman. She had a head like a bird of prey and a long, shrivelled body.

'Go away! Go away! Go away!' she started shrieking at us. 'What do you want here? Aren't we masters even in our own house? Don't you know that we've got a party here today? The banquet to celebrate my husband's appointment takes place in an hour's time, and nobody invited you! My husband isn't at home, and when he does come home he won't have any time to waste on you. If you want to talk to him go and see him at the brickworks!'

The gendarmes showed us the way to the brickworks and then left us.

After losing our way several times we got to the brick-kiln. About twenty workmen were there, and some carters loading bricks, but the Contractor wasn't there. He'd been there a little while ago, but had just left. He might be at the electric sawmill, but most likely he'd been there and gone already. It would be best to go to the tannery. But the tannery was a long way off.

We didn't know what to do, and stopped, undecided, in the middle of the dusty road. The heat was suffocating and the dust got into our eyes. What with dust in our hair, our mouths, our throats and our clothes, we were quite filthy by this time and almost unrecognisable. And we were exhausted with hunger and the heat.

'It's all your fault, damn you, damn you!' Lisabetta Limona burst out at Sorcanera.

This was the signal for a general scuffle. Ponzio Pilato's wife went for me.

'It was you who dragged me here!' she shrieked. 'I didn't

want to come, I've got plenty to do at home, I've got no time to waste out of doors tramping the highways and byways!'

Giuditta Scarpone and Cannarozzo's daughter started tearing each other's hair out, but finished up on the ground. Maria Grazia came to the rescue of Cannarozzo's daughter, but Recchiuta flung herself on top of her, and all four ended up on the ground in a cloud of dust. Fortunately their shrieks were more serious than the blows either given or taken. Sorcanera, in between Zompa's wife and Lisabetta Limona, screamed as if her throat were being cut, but all she lost was a little hair and her new apron that got torn to shreds. The scrap only ended because the kiln-workers came and interfered.

'We did wrong to follow that witch,' Lisabetta said – meaning Sorcanera – when peace was restored. 'I don't suppose the Contractor had anything to do with diverting the stream. What have we come here for, anyway?'

'Let's go and see Don Carlo Magna,' Michele Zompa's wife proposed. 'The stream is being turned towards his land. The whole thing may be a bit of bluff – perhaps he's just trying it on.'

We split up into two or three hostile groups and went back towards the town. We went to Don Carlo Magna's house. The usual servant opened the door. We asked the usual question.

'Can we see Don Carlo for a moment, please?'

We were given the usual answer:

'Don Carlo? *magna*, he's at table just now. Would you like to see madam?'

Madam, who knew us well, came out just at that moment. She received us as if she had been waiting for us. She took us into the big kitchen. Hams, salami, sausages, bladders of lard, clusters of sorb-apples, garlic and onions hung from the ceiling. Donna Zizzola's clothes were always old-fashioned. She wore a black cap and a long, black gown which swept the ground. When she spoke it was as if she were weeping. She couldn't talk without seeming to lament. The wives of our landowners are as well up in matters of business as the men. Their opinions on matters of property and inheritance almost always prevail over those of the men. It is they who look after the family property, manage the servants, pay the workpeople, fix the price at which the produce of their land is to be sold. The landowners' wives, fiercely defending the integrity of the land that came to them as their dowry, are responsible for keeping at least a fraction of the family property safe from their husbands' speculations and debts.

It was common knowledge that, but for the restraining influence of his wife, Don Carlo Magna, a celebrated pleasure-lover, gambler, drinker and eater, would long ago have frittered away his whole inheritance. The maidservant's invariable reply to all callers who asked for Don Carlo was an expedient discovered by the mistress of the house many years ago to keep control of her husband's affairs.

By the time we had finished explaining about the brook Donna Zizzola was as pale as if she were going to faint. Her rigid, fleshless face betrayed the effort she was making to restrain her tears.

'That brigand! That brigand!' she muttered to herself. She didn't mean her husband. She meant the Contractor.

'The man is a real brigand,' she said to us. 'No law restrains him. If he stays here another couple of years, he'll devour us and our houses and land and trees and mountains, too. He'll ruin us all. He and his diabolical bank will drag us all down to the gutter – and when we're begging in the gutter he'll even steal our alms.'

Then she told us that just a week ago the strip of land belonging to Don Carlo Magna to which the Fontamara stream was to be diverted had been bought up cheaply by the Contractor. No doubt after converting it into irrigable land he would sell it and make a large profit on the deal.

'And now they have made him *podestà*,' Donna Zizzola

went on. 'The new Government have made him *podestà*. The new Government is in the hands of a band of brigands. They call themselves bankers, they call themselves patriots, but they are nothing but brigands, with no respect for the old landowners. It's only twenty-four hours since this brigand became *podestà*, and the typewriters have already vanished from the town hall. Inside a month the doors and windows will have gone, too. The street-sweepers are paid by the commune, but from tomorrow on they work as builder's labourers in the Contractor's factory. The roadmen, whose wages come out of the rates, are digging a bed for the stream that is to take the water to the land stolen by that brigand from my husband. Innocenzo La Legge, the district collector, has become the Contractor's wife's servant. I met him this morning, slinking along with his head down like a dog, following behind her with a big basket of vegetables. And this is only the beginning. Before long the brigand will have devoured us all.'

All we gathered from her excited talk was this: that the day of reckoning had come for the old landowners, too. As the old saying goes, as they make their bed so must they lie on it.

So once again we set out to the *podestà*'s villa. My legs were aching from all this walking, as they do on Good Friday when I make the stations of the Cross on my knees. My bare feet hurt, too.

On the way we met Antonio Zappa, a Fontamara goatherd, who was also looking for the Contractor. He had been on the common grazing ground as usual with his goats when a rural guard had come up to him and warned him off, because that part of the grazing ground belonged to the Contractor.

'If the grazing ground belongs to the Contractor, the very air we breathe must belong to him, too,' the goatherd said.

Antonio Zappa wasn't a very bright lad, but this time he was perfectly right. But the rural guard might have been pulling his leg. Grazing grounds have always belonged to everybody, from our mountains to Apulia. In the month of May, after the clothes fair, about a million sheep come to spend the whole summer on our mountains, and they stay there right up to October. This is said to have happened even before the birth of Christ. I don't know how many wars and invasions and changes of popes and kings there have been since then, but the grazing grounds have always been open to everybody.

'The Contractor must be mad if he thinks he can touch a grazing ground,' we said. 'Or perhaps he isn't mad but the rural guards are pulling our leg.'

At the gate of the *podestà*'s villa we found the maid in complete despair.

'The *podestà* hasn't come back yet,' she said. 'The company's been at table for half an hour already, and the most important person hasn't arrived.'

We could smell the cooking from where we were. The maid told us all about the banquet in great detail. Don Circostanza had made a beautiful speech. Then she told us about every single item on the menu – the onions and the sauces and the mushrooms and the potatoes and all the flavours and savours, too.

The banquet must have been nearing its end, because the effect of the wine was already beginning to make itself felt. We could hear Don Circostanza's voice above all the rest. Snatches of talk came through the wide-open windows.

At one point a violent argument broke out about the Almighty. Don Abbacchio and the chemist were on opposite sides. Don Circostanza's opinion was asked.

'The Almighty?' he said. 'Why, it's obvious! The Almighty is an adjective!'

Everybody agreed with this, and peace was restored.

Then we heard the drunken voice of Don Abbacchio.

'In the name of bread, sausage and good white wine, amen!'

A burst of laughter greeted this witticism.

Another pause. Then, in his most ecclesiastical voice, Don Abbacchio intoned: '*Ite, missa est.*'

This was the sign to rise from table.

The guests started coming out into the garden to relieve nature.

The first was Don Abbacchio, fat and puffing, the veins on his neck swollen, his red face bloated, his eyes half-closed in an expression of hog-like bliss. He was so drunk that he could hardly stand upright, and he started making water against a tree. He leaned his head against the tree to prevent himself from falling, with his open breeches towards us.

Next came Don Pomponio, the lawyer, with the sergeant of gendarmes holding him up. He, however, had the decency to go behind the house where nobody could see him.

Next came the chemist, the tax-collector, the postmaster and the notary, who proceeded to relieve nature behind a pile of bricks.

The next was the lawyer, Don Ciccone, with a young man holding him up by the arm. He started being sick behind the tree that Don Abbacchio had previously watered, while the young man held his head with one hand.

The next was an old town-hall clerk, known as the Student, because he'd had himself entered at the university at the age of twenty, and at the age of sixty was still working for his exams. He went behind the house.

The next was the lawyer, Don Cuccavascio, small and fat, with the eyes of an ox and the jaws of a horse, who relieved himself behind the pile of bricks.

The next was the lawyer Tarandella, also known as the Bald, because he had no hair on his head, no eyebrows, no eyelashes, no moustache and no beard. We were quite curious to see whether Tarandella was also hairless in another place, too, but unfortunately he went behind the house. The next was the Thinker, who wandered vaguely – lord knows what he was thinking about – all over the garden before using the pile of bricks. He was dead drunk, and we saw him fall on his knees behind the pile of bricks in his own water. While he was still thinking out the best way to get up, the maid, who had been with us outside the gate on the look-out for the return of the Contractor, suddenly saw him coming.

He was carrying on a lively conversation with a number of workmen. He was in his ordinary workaday clothes, his jacket over one arm, a spirit-level in his hand, and a ruler sticking out of his trouser-pocket. His shoes were burnt with lime, and his trousers and shoulders dirty with lime and plaster. Nobody who did not know him would have believed he was the richest man in the whole province and head of the commune. Although he noticed our presence he went on shouting and arguing with the workmen.

'If the carter isn't careful and goes on breaking tiles I'll make him pay for the damage,' he shouted. 'What? He wants to be paid for last month? The audacity of the man! Is he frightened I'll run away? Instead of being grateful to me for giving him work in these hard times . . . What! the cement-workers don't want to work ten hours a day? Really? I work twelve hours a day. I'm the boss, and I work twelve hours a day!

'Rosalia,' he started shouting towards the villa. His wife immediately appeared on the veranda. 'Has the architect brought the plans? What? Does the man suppose I pay him for filling his belly? Has the station-master brought that bill of lading? What? Do you mean to tell me he hasn't? That fellow will have to be transferred to Calabria. Has the chief of police been here? . . . What? You sent him away? What did you send him away for? . . . The banquet? What banquet? . . . Oh, the one to celebrate my appointment . . . I'm sorry, I've got no time, I've got to go and see the chief of police . . . What? The guests will be offended? Oh, no, they won't. Give them drinks, I know them, give them plenty of drinks and they won't be offended . . . oh, nonsense, I know them.'

And then he passed right in front of the villa gate, without so much as a glance at us, and went on arguing with the workmen he was with. His way of talking and doing things was positively awe-inspiring.

'Really,' I said to myself. 'If that brigand stays here another two years, he'll be the cock of the whole roost.'

'Wait here, you women,' Antonio Zappa shouted, and ran after him.

We saw him disappearing behind a house that was being built and waited for him to come back.

Meanwhile the drunken guests had gathered on the veranda.

Don Circostanza, with his great, warty nose and protruding ears, stood out among the other lawyers. His belly was at the third stage. It is well known that lawyers in our part of the world wear special trousers to go to banquets in. They are known as concertina or academic trousers because instead of one row of buttons they have three, so that they can be let out gradually in accordance with bodily needs. The first stage, as a rule, is reached with the entree, the second with the roast, and the third with the dessert.

That day the concertina trousers of Don Circostanza, Don Pomponio, Don Ciccone, Don Cuccavascio and the Student were all at the third stage.

As soon as Don Circostanza saw us he shouted a noisy greeting.

'Long live my Fontamaresi!' he shouted.

Don Circostanza had always had a special partiality for the people of Fontamara. All their lawsuits used to pass through his hands. For this reason most of the eggs and chickens of Fontamara used to find their way eventually to Don Circostanza's kitchen. Once upon a time, when only those who could read and write had the right to vote, a writing-master came to Fontamara and taught all the peasants to write Don Circostanza's Christian name and surname. So the people of Fontamara always voted solidly for him, because they wouldn't have been able to vote for anybody else even if they'd wanted to. Later on elections were given up, and not one of us went into mourning on that account.

But Don Circostanza still kept the title of the People's Friend.

'The presence of these excellent women from Fontamara enables us to complete the telegram we have decided to send to the Head of the Government,' Don Circostanza said to the gentlemen who were with him on the veranda.

He took a piece of paper out of his pocket, wrote something down and then read out at the top of his voice:

'Authorities and people, united in brotherly concord, applaud the appointment of the new *podestà*.'

When we saw that the Contractor wasn't coming back and that the guests were saying goodbye to his wife, and were going away without anybody having taken any notice of us at all, we lost our patience. We stood across the gateway, determined not to let anyone pass until we'd been given a hearing and an assurance that the stream would not be diverted. We started making an uproar.

'You ought to be ashamed of yourselves, treating poor people like this! Robbers! Thieves! We've been on our feet since early this morning without anyone taking any notice of us! God will chastise you! God will punish you!'

Two or three of us picked up stones and threw them at a window on the first floor. The glass broke. At the sound of the breaking glass we dashed to a pile of bricks next to the gate. The drunks in the garden on their way out were terrified and fled back to the villa for refuge. The maid hastily closed the shutters on the top floors.

Suddenly we heard the Contractor's voice behind us. His voice was perfectly calm.

'What are you doing with my bricks?' he asked us. 'Those bricks belong to me, and you can't take them, even to stone me with,' he said. 'Besides, there's no need to stone me. I'm here to give you any explanations you want.'

We put the bricks back and entered the villa garden. We

stood on one side and the Contractor and his drunken guests, all of whom had not yet overcome their fear, on the other.

Marietta Sorcanera advanced, placed one hand on her heart, just at the height of the medal, and in carefully chosen words described the wickedness of the road-menders who wanted to divert the course of the Fontamara stream.

'We are sure your worship will punish the roadmenders for their presumption,' Marietta concluded.

'If it were presumption, you may be sure that I would take measures to suppress it,' the Contractor answered. 'As long as I'm head of the commune there won't be any presumption, especially against workers like the people of Fontamara. You may rest assured of that. But in this case there's no question of presumption. Captain, explain what it's all about.'

The captain of the gendarmes advanced from the group of guests.

'There's no question of presumption,' he said. 'Under the new Government presumption cannot possibly occur. On the contrary, it's a legal act. It's actually a favour the authorities have granted the inhabitants of Fontamara.'

He took a bundle of papers from his pocket and continued.

'Here is a petition signed by all the inhabitants of Fontamara. This petition, which was signed by every single inhabitant, without any exceptions, asks the Government, in the interests of increased production, to divert the stream from the insufficiently cultivated land belonging to the Fontamaresi towards the fields belonging to the town, whose proprietors can devote more capital to its exploitation.'

The captain wanted to say more, but we wouldn't let him. We knew perfectly well how a certain Hon. Pelino had written down the names of the people of Fontamara on blank sheets of paper the night before.

'Swindlers! Forgers! Cheats!' we started yelling. 'You only study the laws to swindle the poor! Down with false petitions!'

The Contractor tried to get a word in, but couldn't.

'We won't hear any more,' we shrieked. 'All your speeches are traps! No more arguments! The water is ours and ours it will remain! We'll set fire to the villa! Burn it down! Burn it down!'

Don Circostanza came to the Contractor's rescue.

'These women are perfectly right!' he started shouting. 'They are right, ten times right, a hundred times right, a thousand times right...'

We stopped at once. Don Circostanza had started defending us, and we knew he was a great lawyer.

'These women are perfectly right,' the People's Friend went on. 'They are ten thousand times right. I have always defended them and I always shall! What is it, at bottom, that these women are asking for? They are asking to be respected...'

'Hear, hear! Hear, hear!' a number of us interrupted.

'They are asking to be respected, and it is our duty to give them our respect, because they are worthy of it. These women are not presumptuous. They have understood that the law is against them, and they don't want to go against the law. What they want is a friendly agreement with the podestà. They are appealing to his goodness of heart. They are appealing, not to the head of the commune, but to the public benefactor, the philanthropist, the friend of the people, who has given everything to his country without taking anything from it. Is an agreement on these terms possible? Of course it is...

When Don Circostanza had finished making his speech, a number of compromises were suggested. Don Abbacchio made one, the notary another, the tax-collector a third. They were all impossible, because they did not take into account the quantity of water required for irrigation.

The Contractor didn't say anything. He let the others talk.

Don Circostanza found the real solution.

'These women say that half the stream is not sufficient to irrigate their fields. That is, if I rightly interpret their wishes, they want more than half. They are right, ten times right. There's one solution and one solution only. The *podestà*. must be left three-quarters of the water of the stream, and three-quarters of the water that's left must be preserved for the people of Fontamara. In other words, they'll have three-quarters each, that is, a little more than half each. That is the only possible way out. I realize that my proposal inflicts an enormous hardship on the *podestà*, but I appeal to him as philanthropist and public benefactor, accustomed to give and not to take.. . .'

Don Ciccone, Don Cuccavascio, Don Tarandella, Don Pomponio and the captain, having by this time recovered from their fright, surrounded the Contractor and implored him to make this sacrifice on our behalf. After a little reflection the Thinker joined them, too.

After a lot of persuasion the Contractor gave in.

Somebody brought a piece of paper.

The notary wrote down the terms of the compromise and made the Contractor sign it. The captain of the gendarmes signed it, and Don Circostanza signed it too, as the representative of the people of Fontamara.

After that we all started walking home.

(As a matter of fact not one of us understood what the agreement really amounted to.)

My husband will tell you what happened next.

3   During the next few days an escort of two gendarmes was provided for the roadmen at work on the trench
that was going to divert part of our stream to the land
bought up by the Contractor. Exactly what part wasn't at all
clear.

We weren't nearly well educated enough to understand
how the stream could possibly be divided into two parts of
three-quarters each. The women who had accepted the terms
were by no means agreed as to how it would work out in
practice. Some thought that the water would be divided into
two equal parts, others that Fontamara would get more than
half, in other words, three-quarters. General Baldissera stout-
ly maintained that the three-quarters referred to the phases
of the moon. By this he meant that during three lunar phases
the stream would irrigate the land of the people of
Fontamara and during the three following phases the land
belonging to the Contractor, and so on.

Every single one of us realised that it would have been
sheer waste of time to try to go on fighting the Contractor.
Each one of us was far more eager to establish his claim, at

the expense of all the rest, to as large a share as possible of what little water there would be left. The time for irrigation was still some weeks ahead, but squabbles and rows began right away.

At that time most of us were going to the Fucino each day to work. We had to get up at about three o'clock and be at the market-place in the local town before dawn and wait there until someone offered us work for the day. At one time only the very poorest peasants had had to do this, but now bad times had come for everybody. Every peasant owned a small strip of land, but it was mortgaged and hardly yielded enough to pay the interest on the debt. The landowners and big farmers took advantage of the larger numbers of peasants that now came to the market-place to cut the wages, but however low they were there was always someone hungry enough to accept them. Many got to the point of offering their labour without first settling how much they were to be paid, so eager were they for any miserable pittance.

You had to walk between five and ten miles from the market-place to the Fucino, according to the exact spot where you were going to work. This was on top of the three miles you had walked from Fontamara to the town. The same walk had to be repeated to get home in the evening. Every day, on the way to Fontamara and back, quarrelling over the division of the water became more violent.

Several men were seriously injured. A cut with Giacobbe Losurdo's bill-hook cost Michele Zompa nearly the whole of one buttock. Baldovino Sciarappa had his head split open like a water-melon. Antonio Ranocchia had his arm broken by his brother-in-law. Things looked uglier still between Ponzio Pilato and me, because neither of us was inclined to give in and both of us went ostentatiously to work accompanied by our sons, all armed as heavily as possible. We didn't even greet each other when we met, but the way we looked at one another was a kind of mutual assurance that the day of reckoning could not be indefinitely postponed.

I met him one morning when I was going to the Fucino with my son. He was talking to the road-menders.

'Look here,' he said. 'The water must be left for my beans. To hell with everything else!'

'To hell with you first!' I shouted, rushing at him with a bill-hook in each hand.

Berardo Viola and the two gendarmes who were on duty with the roadmen were watching, so there was no slaughter that time.

For some days Berardo came with me to the Fucino every day, in order to avoid a meeting with Ponzio Pilato. He was able to act as keeper of the peace in this matter of the water for the simple reason that he owned no land himself, so his interests didn't clash with anybody else's.

He had sold the only bit of land his father had left him a few years before, intending to emigrate to America, but the permission to emigrate had never come, and so he had stayed on at Fontamara, rather like a dog that has escaped from the chain that held it but cannot enjoy its new-found liberty and hankers hungrily after the advantages it has lost. He was far from being a peacemaker by nature.

He was a grandson of the famous brigand Viola, the last brigand in our part of the country, who was caught by the Piedmontese in 1867. Berardo inherited his grandfather's body and spirit. He was almost a giant in size, as sturdy as the limb of an oak tree, with a solid, square head like an anvil, two enormous eyes like those of a man possessed, bold, reckless, impulsive, always ready for a fight, without fear of God or man, fond of wine, extravagant and generous to his friends, but obstinate too. His physical strength gave him great influence over certain young people of Fontamara. This influence had one drawback. It often led to violence and destruction, leading to no practical advantage.

After he received definite notice that he would not be allowed to emigrate, the grapes of a whole vineyard belonging to Don Carlo Magna were found cut down one day. In reply to the famous joke of the donkey and the priest, water-pipes leading to the town were broken in various places. Another time milestones on the main road were smashed to pieces for a distance of about eight miles. And signposts put up for the benefit of motorists never remained in their place for more than two or three days.

When the electric light failed for the first time at Fontamara, Berardo said nothing, but two nights later all the lights along the road between the town and the neighbouring villages were smashed.

'It's no use arguing with townspeople.' That was the whole doctrine of Berardo Viola.

This is how he would explain it:

'The law is made by townspeople, interpreted by lawyers, who are townspeople, and applied by judges who are townspeople. How can a peasant ever expect justice?'

If anyone asked him whether you shouldn't argue even if they tried to cut your wages, he had a ready answer.

'It's a complete waste of time,' he would say. 'It's a complete and absolute waste of time for a day-labourer to argue with a farmer. He'll get less pay anyway. A farmer acts entirely according to his own interests. The only thing that ever stops a farmer from cutting wages is the fact that it doesn't always pay him. Why doesn't it? I'll tell you why it doesn't. They cut the boys' pay for weeding in the cornfields from seven to five lire. The boys did what I told them and didn't complain, but instead of pulling the weeds out they simply covered them over with earth. After the April rains the farmers noticed that the weeds were higher than the corn. The little they thought they'd gained by cutting the wages they'll lose ten times over in a few weeks' time when it comes to threshing. If they cut the pay for reaping it's no good arguing or complaining. There's more than one way of reaping. There are ten ways. Each way corresponds to a definite rate of pay. If the pay's good the reaping will be good, if the pay's bad the reaping will be bad.'

He would answer in the same way if someone asked him whether we shouldn't complain to the Contractor about the way he'd robbed us of our water.

'Set fire to the tannery, and he'll restore your water without any argument,' he would say. 'And if he doesn't understand, set fire to his timber yard. And if that isn't sufficient, blow up his brickworks. And if he's an idiot and still doesn't understand, burn his villa down one night when he's in bed with Donna Rosalia. That's the only way to get your water back. If you don't, he'll take your daughters and sell them in the market-place one day, too. And I don't blame him either. What are your daughters worth anyway?'

Such was the bitter doctrine of Berardo Viola. But he only argued like that because he owned no land and the lack of it burned him up inside. He argued like a man who had nothing to lose. The other peasants were in a different position.

His plan to emigrate to America and the way he used to work at the most varied jobs according to the season – now day-labourer, now woodcutter, now charcoal-burner, now bricklayer – made it perfectly clear that he was not, at heart, content with his state. And, being landless, and therefore reduced to a lower status than the other peasants, he had no right to presume that anyone would follow his advice. So every time he interfered in any of our arguments he only succeeded in increasing the confusion, and no practical man ever listened to him, even to contradict him. The only exception was General Baldissera, whose point of view was diametrically opposed to his. But being a cobbler he was naturally fond of useless arguments.

But Berardo entirely changed the outlook of the young people of Fontamara by his wild speeches and the example he set.

Never before had there been so many young people at Fontamara. Once upon a time young people used to leave home almost as soon as they were sixteen. Some went to the

Roman Campagna, some to Apulia, others to America. Many would leave their fiancées for four, six, sometimes ten years, and would marry on their return. Others would marry the day before emigrating and would leave home for four, six or even ten years, after just one night together. They would find quite big sons and daughters waiting for them when they came home, and sometimes it happened that there would be several sons and daughters of quite different ages.

But the prohibition of emigration had put a stop to all this, and the young had no choice but to stay at Fontamara, where work was becoming scarcer for everybody. The impossibility of emigrating meant the impossibility of earning and saving the amount that might have enabled them to save the debt and mortgage ridden residue of paternal property, that might have permitted them to introduce the necessary improvements and cultivate the land by less primitive methods, that might have enabled them to replace a dead or ageing ass with a young ass, to buy a pig or two goats, or to buy a bed to enable them to marry. But, being young, they didn't give vent to their discontent in grumbling and complaints. They didn't give any outward sign that they realized the unusual harshness of their lot. They would meet on their frequent days of leisure and, under the influence of the one among them who was the oldest in years but the youngest in intelligence, they would plan and do things that were entirely without rhyme or reason.

In winter they would meet, for preference, in Antonio Zappa's stable, where the breath of the goats warmed the air a little. Antonio Spaventa went there, and Luigi Della Croce and Palummo and Raffaele Scarpone, and Venerdì Santo, and my son and Ponzio Pilato's son and others, too. Berardo Viola would turn up every time anything violent was being organised.

No one else was admitted to this little society, which the girls of Fontamara called the Vice Club. The name was more justified than at first appeared. In fact, it was discovered one day that the favourite hobby of these youths was abusing goats, particularly a young female belonging to Baldovino Sciarappa, called Rosetta because of the colour of her skin. It was said of this animal that she submitted to the men with a great deal of docility and pleasure. There were frequent quarrels about Rosetta, and this abomination went on a long time, because, as so often happens in such cases, Baldovino Sciarappa, the owner of the goat, was the last to hear about it. Because of the scandal many peasants who formerly entrusted their goats to Antonio Zappa would do so no longer, and the Vice Club dissolved.

But the greatest wonder of all was that a healthy and vigorous young man like Berardo, already nearing his thirtieth year and having no father or mother, should put up with living with his grandmother, who was about ninety years old, and show no intention of taking a wife. Once there had been a kind of understanding between him and Elvira La Tintora, and a better match he could not have made, but after the loss of his strip of land Berardo had broken with her, without giving any explanation. Asking him news about Elvira was a sure way of infuriating him. On winter evenings, when there was no work, and the old people would drink and the young make love, Berardo would sit up late and argue with General Baldissera about the differences between townsman and peasant and about the three laws – the priest's law, the boss's law and the law of custom. He would thump the table so hard that Marietta Sorcanera's bar shook. The old general remained unshaken, however, in his partisanship of the 'eternal and unchanging order' of society.

It might have been supposed that Berardo had relinquished all claims to Elvira, but one day when the news spread that Filippo Il Bello, the road-mender, had asked her hand in marriage Berardo burst out like a mad bull. He rushed to Filippo's house but found he was out. Hearing that he was at the quarry, he dashed there and found him busy at the gravel heaps. Without even asking him whether the story about Elvira and him was true, Berardo picked him up as if he were a feather and bumped him on a gravel heap about ten times. Then the other workmen came up and stopped him.

From that day on no one else dared approach Elvira, although Berardo continued avoiding her.

One evening, on the way home from the Fucino, I tried to sound him on the subject.

'Elvira must be over twenty-five now,' I said, 'and that's getting on in our part of the world, where the girls marry before they're twenty. Apart from anything else she ought to get married to have some help about the house.'

Berardo didn't answer.

'If you don't make up your mind to marry her she's got the right to marry somebody else.'

Berardo flew into a rage.

'Shut up,' he said, in a way that put an end to that subject of conversation.

Next day I waited for him in vain before going to the Fucino. I went to his house to see if he were asleep. I found the old woman almost in tears.

'Berardo's going mad,' she said. 'He'll come to a worse end than his grandfather. He didn't sleep a wink all last night, not even for a minute. He got up at about two o'clock. "It's a bit early to go to the Fucino," I said to him. "I'm not going to the Fucino," he said. "Where are you going?" I said. "To Cammarese," he said. "Why are you going to Cammarese if there's work at Fucino?" "There's more money at Cammarese," he said. "Since when did you care about money?" I said. But off he went without another word. '

The news of Berardo's departure for Latium spread quickly and amazed the peasants of Fontamara, though there's no earthly reason why a peasant who lives by day-labouring should stay in his own district, even when the season's work is at its height, if he can earn more money anywhere else. Our amazement was all the greater when Berardo returned to

Fontamara the same evening.

Four or five of us, including Marietta and General Baldissera, were standing in the middle of the street, talking about him, as it happened. When we saw him turn up so unexpectedly, we thought for a moment that the news of his departure must have been a joke. But we saw that he was wearing his best shirt and hat, and carrying a bundle under his arm. What on earth was he coming back for? He told a very confused story.

'I was at the station. I had my ticket. A squad of gendarmes came and started asking everyone for their papers and wanted to know why they were travelling. I told them the truth straight away. I said I was going to Cammarese to work. They answered: "Well, where are your papers?" "What papers?" I said. "You can't work without papers," they said. But what papers? I couldn't get a proper explanation. They made me go to the booking-office and get the money for my ticket back and then they turned me out of the station. So I decided to go on foot to the next station and take the train from there. As soon as I'd got my ticket two gendarmes turned up and asked me where I was going. I said I was going to Cammarese to work. "Show us your papers," they said. "What papers? What have papers got to do with it?" I said. "You can't work without papers," they said. "There's a new internal migration regulation," they said. I tried to persuade them that my going to Cammarese had nothing whatever to do with internal migration and that all I wanted there was work. But it wasn't any good. "We've got our orders," the gendarmes said. "We can't allow any workman who hasn't got papers to enter a train to go and work in any other district." They made me get the money back for my ticket and turned me out of the station. But I couldn't swallow that story about papers. I went into an inn and got into conversation with some men there. "Papers?" a carter said to me. "How is it you don't know about papers? During the War we hardly ever talked about anything else." And so here I am again, after wasting nearly a whole day.'

The person who was most impressed by Berardo's story was General Baldissera, who produced from his pocket a printed circular he had received by post and said:

'They talk about papers in this, too!'

There was no doubt about it. The Workmen's Federation, Leather Section, Province of Apulia, peremptorily required General Baldissera to obtain cobbler's papers.

'Elvira got a letter just like that, too,' Marietta said. 'She came to me quite frightened and asked me to explain it. I couldn't make head or tail of it. All I could make out is that they've taken away one's freedom to work. All Elvira's fathers and forefathers were dyers and weavers before her, and no one ever interfered with them, but now they've written and told her that if she wants to go on working she must pay a tax and get papers.'

This business of the circular letters and Berardo's adventures all happening at the same time made me suspect that the whole thing was a practical joke.

'What's the Government got to do with dyeing and weaving?' I said. 'Why should the Government interfere with peasants going from one province to another looking for work? Governments have got other things to think about. These things are private affairs entirely. It's only in wartime that governments interfere with people's liberties in this way.'

'What do you know about it anyway?' General Baldissera interrupted. 'How the devil do you know whether we are at peace or at war?'

This question impressed everybody.

'If the Government insists on people having papers it must mean that we are at war,' the General continued lugubriously.

'War with whom?' Berardo asked. 'How could we be at war without knowing anything about it?'

'How can you tell?' said the General. 'How can an ignorant, landless peasant like you possibly be expected to tell? It's the townspeople who declare the wars, but the peasants who fight them. When the last war broke out no one at Fontamara knew whom it was against. Ponzio Pilato thought it was against Menelik, Simpliciano thought it was against the Turks, and it wasn't till years later that we found out it was against the Trentino and Trieste. Nobody has ever been able to find out whom some of the wars in history were against. War? Why, a war is such a complicated thing that a peasant can never hope to understand it. A peasant sees just one little fraction of the war – papers, for instance – and that makes a big impression on him. A townsman sees much more of it – barracks and munition factories and everything. The king sees the whole country. God alone sees all.'

'Well, are you going to get your papers or not?' I asked Baldissera.

'Oh, yes, I'll get my papers all right, but I shan't pay for them,' he said.

Whatever we might say about it, we were in agreement about one thing – the attitude we were all going to adopt to this question of papers.

There was a lot more talk about war that night. There wasn't a household in which it wasn't talked about. Everyone asked everybody else: 'Whom is the war against?' and nobody knew. General Baldissera, seated in front of Sorcanera's bar, patiently answered everyone who came to him for information.

'Whom we are fighting against? I haven't the slightest idea,' he said. 'There wasn't anything about it in the circular I got. All it said was that you had to pay a fee for your papers.'

What most of the peasants said was: 'Pay, pay, pay, it's pay all the time.'

The unexpected arrival of Innocenzo La Legge increased the general bewilderment.

Innocenzo must have had a very serious reason indeed for

coming back to Fontamara. An only too well justified fear for his own skin had kept him away for some months. He certainly hadn't come of his own free will. He had a moment of panic when he arrived in front of Sorcanera's inn and the peasants rushed up to him and surrounded him. His livid face betrayed his terror. Sorcanera gave him a stool just in time to save him from collapsing.

'Excuse me, excuse me,' he said, in a thin little trickle of a voice. 'No, don't be frightened, no, don't be frightened, there's nothing whatever to be frightened of, is there? You're not frightened of me, are you? . . . '

'Come on, tell us what it's all about,' Berardo said in a tone that wasn't very encouraging.

'Very well, let's come to the point right away. It's nothing whatever to do with taxes. I swear to you by everything that's holy that it's nothing whatever to do with taxes. It's nothing whatever to do with taxes; may God strike me blind if it's anything to do with taxes!'

There was a pause for some moments. Innocenzo was not stricken with blindness.

'Get on with it!' Berardo said.

'Well, look here, you remember that one night an officer of militia came here. The Hon. Pelino his name was, wasn't it? You remember? Good, I'm glad. Well, the Hon. Pelino made a report to the authorities in which he said that Fontamara was a hotbed of enemies of the present Government... Don't be alarmed, there's no harm in that, there's no need to be alarmed at that. The Hon. Pelino reported word for word certain speeches, made here in his presence, against the present Government and the Church. There's no doubt whatever that he didn't understand what you said properly. But the authorities have decided to take certain steps in regard to Fontamara. Nothing serious, I assure you, it'll cost you absolutely nothing at all. It's all a lot of nonsense, the kind of nonsense they attach great importance to in towns, and sensible peasants don't take any notice of whatever. . .'

Innocenzo didn't know all the measures that the authorities had taken against Fontamara. He was only the district collector, and all he knew was the decision made locally by the commune, which it was his job to communicate to those concerned.

He knew nothing about anything else, nor did he want to know anything. The first decision he had to communicate to Fontamara concerned the imposition of the curfew. Everyone at Fontamara would have to be indoors one hour after vespers and stay there till dawn.

'And we'll get our pay just the same?' Berardo asked.

'What's your pay got to do with it?' Innocenzo answered.

'What's it got to do with it? Why, if we can't leave home till dawn we can't get to the Fucino, where we work, till just before noon,' Berardo explained. 'If we're to get the same pay for a couple of hours' work as we did before, three cheers for the curfew!'

'And what about our irrigation? How can we irrigate our fields at night if we've all got to stay at home all night?'

Innocenzo La Legge was nonplussed for a moment.

'You haven't understood properly,' he said. 'Or, if you don't mind my saying so, you pretend not to have understood, just to annoy me. Whoever said that you've got to change your way of living? The Contractor is *podestà* now and you can't stop him doing his job. And I'm district collector and you can't stop me doing mine. To put a stop to protests and complaints from the higher authorities, the Contractor has decided that you've got to stay at home at night. All I've done is to bring you his orders. You must do what seems best to you.'

'And what about the law?' General Baldissera started shouting. 'What's to become of law and order if things go on like this? Is the law the law or not, I ask you?'

'Excuse me,' Innocenzo said, 'what time do you go to bed at night?'

'As soon as it gets dark,' answered the half-blind cobbler.

'And what time do you get up in the morning?'

'About ten, because there's so little work about.'

'Very well, then, I appoint you to see that the law is carried out,' said Innocenzo.

We all started laughing, except Baldissera, who didn't like it a bit. As it was dark by this time he went home to bed. Innocenzo was delighted at the unexpected laugh he'd got, and recovered a little of his self-possession. He lit a cigarette, and started smoking in a way we'd never seen before. Instead of breathing out the smoke, he held it in his mouth and breathed it out through his nostrils, not, as we do, through both nostrils, but first through one nostril and then through the other. He took advantage of our moment of surprise and admiration to impart to us the second of the *podestà*'s decisions about Fontamara. This was to the effect that the following notice was to be put up in every public place in the village:

POLITICAL DISCUSSIONS
FORBIDDEN HERE

by Order

The only public place at Fontamara was Marietta's bar, so Innocenzo handed to her an order, written by the *podestà*, to the effect that she would be held responsible if any more political discussions took place at Fontamara.

'But nobody in Fontamara even knows what politics are,' Sorcanera said, truthfully. 'No one has ever talked politics in my bar.'

'Then what made the Hon. Pelino go back to town in such a rage? What did you talk about?'

'Oh, we talked about all sorts of things,' Sorcanera said. 'We talked about prices and wages and taxes and laws. Today we talked about papers and the war and emigration. . .'

'You mustn't talk about any of these things any more, by order of the *podestà*,' Innocenzo explained. 'The order wasn't specially made for Fontamara, the same thing applies to the whole of Italy. It is absolutely forbidden to discuss prices, wages, taxes and laws in public places.'

'You mean it's forbidden to discuss anything at all?' Berardo said.

'Exactly, Berardo, you've seen the point perfectly; it's forbidden to discuss anything at all. That is the significance of the *podestà*'s decision. No more discussions of any kind.'

Innocenzo's satisfaction at Berardo's agreeing with him was enormous. He readily accepted Berardo's suggestion to amend and make clearer the notice that was to hang on the wall. He himself wrote out, on a large piece of white cardboard:

ALL DISCUSSION STRICTLY
PROHIBITED

by order of the Podestà

Berardo supervised the placing of this notice high up on the wall outside Sorcanera's bar. His compliance in all this absolutely amazed us. As if he hadn't made his attitude clear enough, he said:

'Anyone who touches that notice had better look out!'

Innocenzo held out his hand to him and wanted to embrace him. But Berardo's explanation somewhat damped his enthusiasm.

'Haven't I always told you so? But you had to wait till the *podestà* made a law of it,' he said. 'My principle has always been: never argue with the owners. Arguing and discussing are at the bottom of all the peasants' misfortunes. The peasant is a donkey, a donkey that argues. That's why we're far worse off than real donkeys who never argue, or at any rate pretend not to. Your real donkey will carry fifty, seventy, a hundred pounds, not more; but he doesn't argue. Your donkey will travel at a certain speed and no faster, but he doesn't argue. Your donkey needs a certain quantity of straw and won't take less, but he doesn't argue. You can't get from a donkey what you can get from a cow or a goat or a horse. No argument will convince him, and no speech will move him. He just doesn't understand – or pretends not to. The peasant, on the other hand, will argue. You can persuade him to work beyond the limits of his strength. You can persuade him to go without his meals. You can persuade him to die for his master. You can persuade him to go to war. You can even make him believe that there's such a place as hell. Look at the consequences. Just look at the consequences all round you.'

What Berardo said was nothing new to us, but it terrified Innocenzo La Legge.

'Your donkey won't put up with missing his meals. He says: if I get my food I work; if I don't get my food I don't work. Or rather he doesn't say anything of the sort, because he doesn't argue, but he acts that way quite naturally. Just imagine what would happen if the six thousand peasants who cultivate the Fucino, instead of being donkeys who argue, in other words donkeys you can tame, talk round, bully with gendarmes and priests and judges – just suppose they were real donkeys who couldn't argue at all. Prince Torlonia would have to beg for his living. That was a nice, dark road you came along, my good Innocenzo, and very soon you'll be going home the same way. What prevents us from killing you? Answer me that!'

Innocenzo tried to stammer something in reply, but couldn't. He looked as pale as death.

'What stops us is that, not being donkeys, we argue, and know the consequences of murder. But you wrote on that notice-board in your own hand, Innocenzo, that from today onwards all arguing is forbidden, by order of the *podestà*. You've cut your own throat. . .'

'I say, look here,' Innocenzo managed to say. 'You say you're against arguing, but it seems to me, if you'll excuse my saying so, that you argue too much. Your whole speech is nothing but an argument. I've never heard any kind of donkey talk like that!'

'If all the arguments are in favour of the authorities and the owners,' I asked Berardo, 'why did the *podestà* forbid all kinds of argument?'

Berardo remained silent for a moment. Then he said:

'Oh, well, it's late. I've got to get up at three in the morning to go to the Fucino. Good night!'

And off he went.

Arguments with Berardo always ended like that. He would go on talking for hour after hour, just like a preacher, saying the most absurd and violent things that came into his head, in a tone of voice that did not admit of any answer. Then, when he'd finished and someone asked a question, he'd be completely at a loss and would go away without making any reply.

That night Innocenzo La Legge did not return to town. Perhaps it was Berardo's threatening words, perhaps he suddenly felt a bit unwell. Anyway he spent the night with Sorcanera.

4 Towards the middle of June the news went round that the representatives of the peasants of the Marsica were going to be summoned to Avezzano to hear what the new Government in Rome had decided about the Fucino question.

This piece of news caused a great sensation, because no previous Government had ever been known to admit that there was such a thing as a Fucino question; and, since elections had been given up, even the lawyers in our part of the world had forgotten its existence, though previously they had talked a lot about it.

There could be no doubt that there was a new Government in Rome, because from time to time we heard talk about it. It seemed to be a confirmation that there had been a war, or that there was going to be a war, because war is the only thing that can turn out an old government and let in a new one. Thus the Bourbons replaced the Spaniards in our part of the world, and the Piedmontese the Bourbons. But nobody at Fontamara knew yet where the new Government came from or what its nationality was.

Governments are things that happen in cities.

When there is a change of government all that a poor peasant can say is: 'May the Lord send us a good one,' just as when clouds appear on the horizon in summer it depends not on the poor peasant but on the will of God whether they are the harbingers of rain or hail.

It was very remarkable, however, that a representative of the new Government should want to talk things over on equal terms with the poor peasants.

'We're going back to the old regime,' General Baldissera went about saying. 'In the old days there wasn't a great forest of barracks and sub-prefectures and prefectures like there is now in between the palace and the peasant's hut, and once a year the rulers would disguise themselves as poor people, and go among them at the fairs, listening to their grievances. Then came elections and put a gulf between the rulers and the peasants. But now, if the rumours are true, we are returning to the old regime, from which we should never have departed. . .'

Michele Zompa had the same hope.

'A government based on elections is always controlled by the rich, who work the elections their own way,' he said. 'A government of one man can frighten the rich. Can there be jealousy or rivalry between a king and a peasant? The very idea is ridiculous. But there can easily be jealousy between a king and Prince Torlonia.'

What kept Berardo from contradicting the opinion of the rest, in accordance with his usual bad habit, was the hope that in a redivision of the soil of the Fucino he might be given a share.

'All governments always consist of thieves,' Berardo would argue. 'One thief, of course, is better for the peasants than five hundred. One big thief, however large his appetite, always devours less than five hundred small and hungry thieves. If they're going to divide up the Fucino again, Fontamara must exercise its rights.'

One Sunday morning a motor-lorry arrived at Fontamara, and the driver invited all the peasants who wanted to go to Avezzano to get on board. There would be nothing to pay. The lorry was all decorated with tricolour flags. The authorities had sent it, and we found it astonishing that there was nothing to pay.

It was by mere chance that there were ten or a dozen of us left at Fontamara. The rest had gone to work. The Church has always allowed us to work on Sundays in the summer, when there is a lot to do. But not one of us blamed the new Government for not knowing that reaping begins at the end of June. How can a government of townspeople be expected to know that that is the reaping season? We were quite willing, however, to lose a day's work for the sake of attending a meeting at which the Fucino question was going to be settled.

We of Fontamara have always claimed that we ought to have the right to rent pieces of land at the Fucino, but the Torlonia administration would never allow it, preferring to let the land to doctors, lawyers, professors and rich farmers, who exploited our labour. But we had never altogether given up hope of hiring some land at the Fucino. Our only hope had been to await the famous expropriation of the soil, of which Don Circostanza had so often talked to us, especially at election times.

'The Fucino for those who till its soil!' had been Don Circostanza's slogan.

The Fucino must be taken away from Prince Torlonia and the rich farmers and lawyers and other amateurs, and given to those who cultivated it. That meant the peasants. So the news that the Fucino was going to be divided up threw us all into a great state of excitement, particularly now the Government had sent a special lorry to enable the peasants of Fontamara to take part in the ceremony. The few of us who happened to be at Fontamara climbed into the lorry without asking any questions. Besides me there were Berardo

Viola, Antonio Zappa, Teofilo Della Croce, Baldovino Sciarappa, Simplicio, Giacobbe Losurdo, Ponzio Pilato and his son, Andrea Caporale, and Raffaele Scamorza.

But before we left the driver asked: 'What about your pennant?'

'What pennant?'

'My instructions say definitely that every group of peasants must carry a pennant,' the driver said.

'But what is a pennant?' we asked.

'A pennant is a flag,' the driver explained.

We were anxious not to make a bad impression on the new Government, particularly at the ceremony at which the Fucino question was going to be settled. Teofilo, who kept the keys of the church, suggested that we should take the banner of San Rocco with us, and we agreed. So he went to the church to fetch it, with the help of Raffaele Scamorza. But when the driver saw them coming back, carrying, with great difficulty, a pole fifteen yards long, to which was attached an enormous blue and white flag with a picture of the saint and a dog licking his wound on it, he said he wouldn't take it on his lorry. But it was the only flag we had at Fontamara, and Berardo put his foot down. So the driver finally gave in and agreed to allow us to bring it.

It was an enormous strain. When the lorry was moving three of us had to take turns at keeping the pole erect. Our banner felt more like the mast of a sailing ship in a gale. It must have been visible from a great distance. We saw peasants working in the fields gesticulating in amazement. Women went down on their knees and made the sign of the Cross.

As we approached the first village on the way to Avezzano the driver said to us:

'Sing the anthem!'

'What anthem?' we asked.

'My orders are: In passing through every inhabited place the peasants are to sing the anthem and show signs of great enthusiasm.'

But we didn't know any anthems, and anyway we were far too busy holding aloft the banner of San Rocco.

On the main road we met other lorries full of peasants, and carriages and motor-cars and motorcycles and bicycles, all going to Avezzano too.

The sight of our enormous blue and white banner caused first astonishment and then endless roars of silly laughter. The flags that all the others were carrying were black, no bigger than a pocket handkerchief, with a skull and cross-bones in the centre like those you see on telegraph poles with the inscription: 'Very dangerous.'

There was a scuffle at the entrance to Avezzano because of that banner. A group of young men in black shirts were standing in the middle of the road waiting for us, and they promptly told us to hand it over. We refused because it was the only one we had. The young men ordered the driver to stop the lorry, and then tried to seize the banner by force. But we had been thoroughly irritated by the jeering we had to submit to from everybody on the way, so we resisted vigorously and several black shirts got a nice grey coating of dust in the roadway.

A crowd of excited, shouting people gathered round the lorry. Many were young men in black shirts, but many others were peasants from villages near Fontamara, who recognised us and shouted greetings at the top of their voices. We stayed quietly where we were, standing round the banner in the lorry, our minds firmly made up not to accept any more insults. Suddenly we saw the fat form of Don Abbacchio approaching us, sweating and panting, with a few gendarme officers. Not one of us doubted that he, a priest, would come to the defence of San Rocco. He did the very reverse.

'Do you think it's carnival time?' he shouted at us. 'Is this the way you compromise the concordat between Church and State? How long are you Fontamaresi going on in your riotous ways?'

Without another word we let the young men in black shirts take our banner. If a priest renounced San Rocco, why should we stay loyal to him, at the risk of compromising our rights to the Fucino?

We were taken to the big market square of Avezzano, where we were given a good position in the shade behind the tribune's palace. Other groups of peasants were standing in rows along the walls of the various buildings surrounding the square. Squads of gendarmes stood between each group of peasants. Gendarmes on bicycles rode across the square in all directions. As soon as a fresh lorry arrived the peasants were made to get out and were escorted by gendarmes to positions round the square where they were cut off from the other groups of peasants.

A gendarme officer crossed the square on a beautiful black horse.

Immediately afterwards a gendarme messenger on a bicycle took round an order to each squad. One gendarme came from each squad and handed on the order to each group of peasants. The order was: 'You may sit down.'

We sat down on the ground. We stayed like that for about an hour. Then another messenger caused a great deal of excitement. A group of high officials appeared at the corner of the square. The gendarmes gave us orders:

'Stand up! Get to your feet! Shout at the top of your voices: Long live the *podestà*! Long live honest government! Long live the government that doesn't rob the poor!'

We got to our feet and shouted at the top of our voices.

'Long live the *podestà*! Long live honest government! Long live the government that doesn't rob the poor!'

The only member of the government-that-didn't-rob-the-poor whom we recognised was the Contractor. As soon as the members of the government-that-didn't-rob-the-poor had gone away we sat down again by permission of the gendarmes.

After a few more minutes another messenger caused still

more excitement.

'Stand up! Get to your feet!' the gendarmes ordered us, 'and shout louder still: Long live the prefect!'

We got to our feet and shouted louder still:

'Long live the prefect!'

The prefect passed in a magnificent motor-car and we sat down again by permission of the gendarmes.

But as soon as we had sat down again the gendarmes made us get up once more.

'Shout louder still! Shout as loud as you possibly can: Long live the minister!' they ordered us.

A large motor-car passed, followed by four men on bicycles, and crossed the square like a flash, while we shouted as loudly as we possibly could:

'Long live the minister! Hurrah!'

Then we sat down again, by permission of the gendarmes. The men on duty were relieved for lunch. We opened our bags and began to eat the bread we had brought with us.

At two o'clock the pantomime began all over again. The minister passed first, then the prefect, then the members of the government-that-didn't-rob-the-poor. Each time we had to get to our feet, show signs of great enthusiasm, and shout.

At last the gendarmes said to us:

'You are free now. You can go.'

The gendarmes had to say it to us again:

'It's all over now. You can go now, or take a walk round Avezzano. But you've only got an hour. In an hour's time you must all have gone.'

'What about the minister and the Fucino question?' we asked, but no one took any notice of us.

We didn't feel like going home without finding out what had happened.

'Come along with me,' said Berardo, who knew his way about Avezzano.

He led us to the gate of a palace which was all decorated with flags.

'We want to talk to the minister,' Berardo said to the gendarmes on duty at the gate.

The gendarmes fell on him as if he'd uttered the most terrible blasphemy and tried to drag him inside the gate. But we held on to him and there was a bit of a tussle. A number of people began running up from inside the palace, among them Don Circostanza, obviously drunk, with his concertina trousers at the third stage.

'Let nobody fail in respect to my Fontamaresi! Treat my Fontamaresi well!' he started shouting. The gendarmes let us alone. Don Circostanza came among us and wanted to embrace us and kiss us one by one.

'We want to talk to the minister,' we told the People's Friend.

'The minister has gone,' he told us.

'We want to know how the Fucino question has been settled,' Berardo added.

Don Circostanza told a gendarme to escort us to Prince Torlonia's offices, where an official explained to us how the Fucino question had been settled.

'So the new Government has settled the Fucino question?' Berardo said.

'Yes, the Fucino question has been settled to the satisfaction of all concerned.'

'Then why weren't we called in? Why were we left outside on the square?' Ponzio Pilato asked.

'The minister couldn't possibly discuss the question with ten thousand peasants. But he discussed it with your representative,' the official replied.

'Who was our representative?'

'The Hon. Pelino, commander of militia.'

'How has the land been divided up? How much of it will be given to the peasants of Fontamara? When does the dividing up take place?' Berardo asked.

'The land will not be divided up,' the official replied. 'The minister and the representatives of the peasants decided that small tenant-farmers must be eliminated. Many of them were granted the land because they were ex-service men but war service is no true economic criterion...'

'Quite true,' Berardo said. 'Having gone to the war doesn't signify that you know how to work the land. The important thing is to know how to work the land. The Fucino to the people who cultivate it. That's Don Circostanza's principle.'

'The minister accepted that principle,' the official replied. 'The Fucino to the people who cultivate it. The Fucino to the people who have the means to cultivate it, and the means to have it cultivated. In other words, the Fucino to the people who have sufficient capital. The Fucino must be freed from the wretched, small tenant-farmers and handed over to the wealthy farmers. Those without great capital resources have no right to rent land in the Fucino.'

'What did our representative say?'

'The Hon. Pelino, representing the peasants, said that in the interests of national production the peasants must be eliminated from the distribution of the rentable land of the Fucino. To achieve this he proposed that the rents of the bigger lessees be diminished and those of the smaller lessees increased by twenty per cent. Payment of rent is to be in kind, especially sugar beet, the price of which will be regulated by Prince Torlonia's administration. Small cultivators who do not grow beet will pay seven hundred lire per hectare. I may add that the proposals of your representative were accepted in their entirety. The peasants who gathered at Avezzano from the whole Fucino basin demonstrated their satisfaction by the magnificent reception they gave the minister, the prefect and the other authorities. Is there anything else you want to know?'

'It's perfectly clear,' we said.

It was perfectly clear.

The streets were full of lights. It was quite late by this time, but the illuminations turned night into day.

(Everything was perfectly clear.)

Avezzano had a strange, afflicted look, like a world just going mad. I saw people enjoying themselves in cafés and inns, dancing, and shouting stupid and senseless things, and I had to make an effort to convince myself that everything that had happened was really true. Was the whole thing a joke, or had they all gone mad without noticing it? I asked myself.

'The townspeople are enjoying themselves, they're happy, they're eating and drinking . . . flaunting it in the faces of the peasants,' Berardo said.

A party of drunken youths passed in front of us, singing to an accompaniment of ribald gestures. The verses were:

My hair and thy hair,
What a lovely wood they'll make . . .

A second group followed the first, and among them were the youths in black shirts who had confiscated the banner of San Rocco on our arrival at Avezzano that morning. As soon as they recognised us they started shouting: 'Hurrah for San Rocco!' and followed that up with a torrent of indecencies. Then they surrounded us, holding hands, and began to dance round us, like a roundabout, singing a song and accompanying it with obscene gestures that were a parody of love. What they sang was:

My legs and thy legs,
What a lovely arch they'll make . . .

We let them do it. We had no spirit to do anything else. We had long ago given up trying to understand. We were in another world, among townsfolk.

The youths left us. They went away singing 'Droll Theresa,' a children's song, to the tune of the 'Hymn to Garibaldi'.

A gentleman came up to us. We noticed that he had been following us for some time. He was well dressed, and he had red hair and a red moustache and a scar on his chin.

'You are from Fontamara?' he said to us.

We didn't answer.

'Do you know that the authorities are frightened of you?' he went on. 'The authorities know that you are against the new Government.'

We let him talk.

'You are undoubtedly in the right,' he continued. 'You are quite right to oppose them. Things cannot go on like this. Come, let us talk things over more quietly.'

The gentleman made for a side turning. We followed him. Behind us walked a young man who, judging by his appearance, seemed to be something between a student and a workman. He smiled at us several times, as if he had something to say to us. The red-haired gentleman led the way to a lonely, deserted café, and we went in behind him. The young man followed us, hesitated a second and then came in after us and took a seat at a table not far from ours.

'Things can't go on like this. Discontent among the peasants is at its height. But you are uneducated. You need someone with education to lead you. Don Circostanza has spoken to me about you with a great deal of sympathy. He wishes you well, but he has to be prudent and he must not compromise himself. If you need me I am entirely at your service. If you have any plans, ask my advice. Do you follow me?'

The unknown gentleman's manner and his way of putting himself entirely at our service would have been suspicious to anyone who had not been in our state of mind. It was the first time that a townsman had ever spoken to us in this confidential way.

We let him talk.

'I understand you,' he said. 'It's enough to look into your eyes to understand you. The gendarmes told you to leave Avezzano within an hour, but you're still here. I understand you. You want to do something against the authorities. It's obvious; you cannot deny it. And why am I here? Why, to help you, to advise you, to sacrifice myself with you. Do you understand?'

We didn't understand in the least. Ponzio Pilato was just going to say something when Berardo nudged him to shut up.

'Very well,' the man went on. 'I am an enemy of the Government, too. Perhaps you want arms; yes, you want to strike a blow against the authorities, but you lack the means, you have no arms. But I tell you that it isn't difficult to find arms, it's easy, it's very easy indeed, nothing in the world could be easier.'

We hadn't spoken a word yet, but the fellow went on asking questions and supplying the answers himself.

'You may say to me: all this sounds very fine, but words are one thing and deeds are another. Very well, put me to the test. Wait here for me for a quarter of an hour and I'll bring you what you want, and, what's more, I'll show you how to use it. Do you still doubt me? Do you still not believe me? Very well, wait for me here.'

He got up, shook hands with us, paid for the wine he had ordered, and went out.

As soon as he had gone the young man sitting at the table next to ours came over to us, and said:

'That was a police spy, an *agent-provocateur*. Be careful. He'll bring you a bomb and then have you arrested. Go away before he comes back.'

We left Avezzano, taking the road across the fields to avoid meeting the *agent-provocateur*.

On foot, thirsty, hungry and full of bitterness, we retraced our steps along the road by which we had come to Avezzano that morning full of hope and with the banner of San Rocco flying in the breeze.

We reached Fontamara about midnight. At three o'clock we were on the road again, walking to the Fucino, for reaping had begun.

5   The commune had had a wooden fence built round the piece of grazing ground that the Contractor had enclosed.

The fence was intended to put an end once and for all to the grumbling of the peasants. The peasants still had some doubts about anyone's right to enclose a piece of land that had been common property for ages, and they went on grumbling about it in spite of the fence.

One day it was burned down.

The Contractor had another fence built at the public expense and put two armed watchmen to guard it.

But could two watchmen intimidate an area that had seen shepherds' quarrels, wolves, brigands and every kind of war and invasion since the day of creation? They could not.

The fence caught fire beneath the very eyes of the two watchmen, who distinctly saw sparks coming out of the earth, followed by flames which burnt down the whole fence in the space of a few minutes. The two watchmen, as is obligatory in the case of every miracle, told the whole story to Don Abbacchio, and then to everybody else who would listen to them. Don Abbacchio, after consulting many old books, decided that the fire was undoubtedly supernatural and had therefore been started by the Devil, so we decided that the Devil could not be so black as he was painted. The Contractor, who couldn't have the Devil arrested, put the two watchmen in gaol instead.

Who would get the best of it, the Devil or the Contractor? We were all against the Contractor, but the only open partisan of the Devil was Berardo Viola.

Some of us Fontamara women were talking it all over one evening at dusk, while waiting in the little square outside the church for our men to return from the Fucino. I was there, and Maria Grazia and Ciammaruga and Filomena and Castagna and Recchiuta and Cannarozzo's daughter, and we were sitting as usual on the little wall that runs along the side of the square facing the valley, like a terrace balustrade. We were looking towards the Fucino, which was already in darkness. The plain below Fontamara, which is divided in two by the dusty streak of the high-road, looked deserted and silent. The branch road that runs from the plain up to Fontamara, winding up the hillside, looked deserted, too.

We knew that our men were going to be late, because at reaping-time at the Fucino they don't work by the clock. Suddenly out of the silence – we didn't notice exactly when it started – we heard a monotonous, rhythmical hum, which first sounded like a beehive and gradually grew and grew until it sounded more like a threshing-machine. The sound came from the plain, but we couldn't make out what was causing it. We couldn't see any threshing-machines. Besides it's only towards the end of reaping-time that threshing machines come anywhere near the high-road.

The noise grew louder and louder.

Suddenly we saw a lorry, full of people, coming round the first bend of the road leading up to Fontamara from the valley. Immediately behind it was a second, and a third, and a fourth, and a fifth.

Five lorries were coming to Fontamara. But immediately behind them there was still another and then more. And then there seemed to be so many that nobody could count them. Were there ten or fifteen or twelve? Cannarozzo's daughter exclaimed that there were a hundred, but then Cannarozzo's daughter can't count. The first lorry had reached the last bend of the road before Fontamara when the last lorry was still at the bottom of the hill. We had never seen so many lorries before. Not one of us had ever imagined that there could be so many lorries.

The whole population of Fontamara – that is to say the women and the old men who hadn't gone to the Fucino – alarmed at the noise made by such an extraordinary number of lorries, rushed out into the little square in front of the church. Everyone had different explanations to offer for the sudden and unexpected appearance of all those motor-lorries.

'It's a pilgrimage! It's a pilgrimage!' Sorcanera exclaimed. Pilgrims don't go on foot nowadays, they go by motor-car! It's a pilgrimage to our San Rocco!'

'No, it's a motor-car race,' said Pasquale Cipolla, who had done his military service in a town. 'A lot of motorists have challenged each other to find out who can go fastest. You see motor-car races in town every day!'

The noise of the lorries grew louder and louder every minute, and then we heard the savage cries of the men who were in them as well. A crackle of sharp explosions, followed by the falling of glass from the window of the church, changed our curiosity to panic.

'They're shooting! They're shooting! They're shooting at the church! They're shooting at us!'

'Get back! Get back!' General Baldissera shouted to us who were nearest the parapet. 'Get back! They're shooting!'

But who were these people who were shooting? Why were they shooting? What were they shooting at?

'It's war! It's war!' General Baldissera started shouting.

'It's war!'

But why war? And why war against us?

'It's war!' the General kept on shouting. 'It's war God knows why, but it's war!'

'If it's war, we must say the war litany,' Teofilo the sacristan said, and began to intone: *Regina pacis, ora pro nobis*, but a second volley struck the facade of the church and spattered us with bits of brickwork. The litany was interrupted. The whole thing seemed absolutely senseless. War? Why should there be a war? Giuditta Scarpone became hysterical. We were like a flock of nanny-goats round her.

We all started shrieking at once. The only one to keep his head was General Baldissera.

'There's no help for it, it's war,' he kept on saying, 'it's war, and there's no help for it; it's war, it's fate. This is what it's always like when war breaks out!'

Maria Vincenza Viola had a good idea.

'Let's ring the church bells,' she said. 'When the country is in danger you ring the church bells. When the Piedmontese arrived in 1860 they rang the church bells all night!'

But Teofilo was so frightened that he couldn't get to his feet. He gave the keys to me. Elvira and I went to the tower to sound the alarm. But Elvira hesitated.

'Has there ever been a war against women?' she asked.

'I've never heard of one,' I told her.

'Well, then, these people that have just arrived haven't come against us but against the men. If they find the men there will be a massacre – there *will* be a war. It's better not to sound the alarm. If we sound the alarm the men will think there's a fire and hurry back and then they'll meet.'

Elvira was thinking of Berardo. I was thinking of my husband and my son. So we stayed in the church tower, without touching the bells.

From the top of the tower we watched the lorries stop at the entrance to Fontamara.

A large number of men, armed with rifles, got out of the lorries. Some stayed near the lorries. The rest came on towards the church.

The people of Fontamara beneath us had finished repeating the litanies and started the supplication:

Propitius esto, parce nobis, Domine,
Propitius esto, exaudi nos, Domine.

Teofilo the sacristan said the supplication, and the others chanted the response: *Libera nos, Domine.* Nobody knew what was going to happen. Teofilo reeled off all the sins he could think of, and after each we answered: *Libera nos, Domine.*

From every evil, *libera nos, Domine,*
From every sin, *libera nos, Domine,*
Ab ira tua, libera nos, Domine,
A subitanea et improvisa morte, libera nos, Domine
A spiritu fornicationis, libera nos, Domine.

Nobody had the slightest idea what was going to happen. Teofilo had got to the supplication against cholera, famine and death when the column of armed men turned the corner into the square, shouting and brandishing their rifles. Their large number dismayed us. Elvira and I drew back instinctively into a corner of the tower, where we could see without being seen.

There must have been about a couple of hundred armed men. Besides their rifles, they had daggers on their belts. They all had black shirts on. The only ones we managed to recognise were the rural guard and Filippo Il Bello, the head road-mender, but the others were not entirely strangers, and did not come from very far away. Some of them were peasants, the landless kind, the kind that go out working for the landlords, earning little and living by sneaking and thieving. Others were dealers, the kind you see hanging round the market-place, and dish-washers and coachmen from private houses and wandering musicians – weak, fawning people, fawning on the big landowners for the privilege of taking it out of the small landowners, unscrupulous lick-spittles, who had once upon a time come to us with orders how we were to vote and now came against us with rifles, making war. Thieves and vagabonds entrusted with the task of defending order and property. Men without family, without honour, without faith, impious, poor and yet enemies of the poor.

A little fat man marched at their head, wearing the tri-colour round his belly. Filippo Il Bello strutted beside him like a turkey-cock.

'What's this you're saying?' the man with the tricolour wound round him said to Teofilo the sacristan.

'I'm praying for peace,' the sacristan answered.

'Very well, I'll give you peace,' the little fat man said, laughing, and beckoned to Filippo Il Bello.

Filippo Il Bello came up to Teofilo and smacked his face.

Teofilo put his hand to his cheek, looked all round him, puzzled, and said:

'What was that for?'

'Coward! Coward! Coward!' the little man began howl-ing. 'Why don't you defend yourself? Coward!'

But Teofilo didn't move or say a word. The little fat man didn't see anyone in the crowd of women and old and sick men before him who looked as if he could be provoked to better effect. After a short consultation with Filippo Il Bello, he said: 'Well, I suppose there's nothing to be done about it.'

Then he turned to the crowd and ordered:

'Go home, everybody.'

When everybody had gone the little man turned to the blackshirts and ordered:

'Split up into groups of five and search every house and confiscate all arms! Quick, before the men come back!'

The square emptied itself like lightning. It was already dark. From our point of vantage we could see the groups of five disappearing into the houses of the few mean streets of Fontamara.

Elvira and I decided that without electric light or anything else to help them these representatives of the law would find it difficult to carry out their search.

But a sudden scream from Maria Grazia, whose house was right next to the church tower, and almost simultaneous screams immediately afterwards from Filomena Castagna, Sofia Recchiuta, Lisabetta Limona, Carracina, Filomena Quaterna and others from houses farther away, together with the rumbling and crashing of overturning furniture, broken chairs and smashed windows revealed to us the real intentions of these armed men.

Maria Grazia, beneath us, was screaming like a beast at the slaughter. Confusedly, through the open door, we could see the struggle of one young woman against five men. Several times she managed to get away and struggle as far as the door, but each time they managed to stop her. They seized her by the legs and shoulders and threw her to the ground and held her while they tore every shred of clothing from her body. Four of them held her arms and legs while the fifth had his will of her. Maria Grazia's screams were like those of an animal whose throat is being cut. When the first man had finished another took his place, and the martyrdom began all over again. And when he had finished it was the third man's turn, and then the fourth man's. But the woman's cries were by this time becoming so feeble that we could hardly hear them. She no longer gave any signs of struggling. The fourth and the fifth took her without there being any need for anyone to hold her arms and legs. When they had finished the men left the house, roaring with laughter, and went to the house of Lisabetta Limona, which was twenty yards farther along.

Elvira had seen the whole thing at my side. There was no way of preventing it. The whole thing had happened only a few yards away, beneath our very eyes. She didn't miss a single detail. I felt her shaking all over, like someone with convulsions, as she clung to me with her arms around my neck.

It was as if the church tower were trembling and the whole earth about us were quaking. I needed all my strength to prevent Elvira from falling, for she might have tumbled down the wooden stairs and revealed our hiding-place. Elvira was still gazing, with enormous, sinister, motionless eyes at the room which the five men had just left, where Maria Grazia's poor tortured body lay. I feared she might lose her reason. I closed her eyes with my hands, as one does to the dead. Then all of a sudden the strength went out of me, my legs collapsed beneath me and everything grew dark.

I don't remember anything else of what happened that night. I only remember what I have told you.

Sometimes it seems to me as if there is nothing else in the whole world that I can remember, except the things that happened that night, which I have just told you. That is how it seems to me sometimes. My husband will tell you the rest.

We men coming back from the Fucino didn't know anything about all this, of course. It was a pity they didn't ring the church bells.

Berardo Viola and Vincenzo Scorza, Papasisto, Ciro Zironda, Maria Grazia's father and Lisabetta Limona's fiancé and I had met on the way home near Pescina, and were coming along together. Giacinto Barletta, Quintiliano, Venerdì Santo, Luigi Serpa and others were following behind.

When we saw the group of armed men and the large number of lorries just outside the village, Berardo said:

'I suppose it's about the fence. I expect the Contractor thinks someone from Fontamara burnt down the fence.'

Several of the armed men standing by the lorries knew Berardo well, but they wouldn't tell us why they had come to Fontamara, or perhaps they didn't know. They just told us to wait, and when the men following behind came along they escorted us all into Fontamara, where we found the armed men drawn up in square formation, with the man with the little fat belly in command, seconded by Filippo Il Bello, the road-mender.

In the middle of the square we saw General Baldissera, Teofilo the sacristan, Pasquale Cipolla, old Antonio Braciola, Anacleto the tailor and a few others, standing silent, motionless, pale and resigned, looking like prisoners of war.

On our arrival the square opened, and closed again as soon as we were inside it.

Berardo looked at me as if he didn't know whether to laugh or be angry. We tried to get from General Baldissera some idea of what had happened before our arrival. All he did was to come near me and whisper in my ear: 'It's absolutely unheard of and then he went up and said it to Berardo, and then he did the same to the others, too. 'It's unbelievable; it's absolutely unheard of,' he said. This remark wasn't very clear, but it was extraordinary coming from Baldissera, who always had an example from history ready to cap even the gravest events.

The square of armed men opened again and admitted a third group of men returning from the Fucino.

These were Ponzio Pilato, Giacobbe Losurdo, Michele Zompa, Giovanni Testone, Giovanni Uliva, Gasparone and a few youngsters.

They looked at us as if we were the cause of all the trouble, but they didn't say anything in the presence of so many armed men.

The next to arrive to keep us company inside the square were Achille Piunzo, Alberto Saccone, Palummo, Recchiuta's husband, Cesidio Verdone and a few more youngsters, including Maria Grazia's fiancé.

Nobody could make out what was happening. Nobody said anything. Everybody looked at everybody else. Everybody realised that something was up between us and the authorities, but no one wanted to compromise himself more than the others. Every man thought first of himself.

The square of armed men opened once more to let in

91

Antonio Spaventa, Raffaele Scarpone, Luigi Della Croce, Antonio Zappa and some others.

It was difficult to imagine what the little fat man was after. Did he want to take us all to prison? It was very unlikely, and practically impossible, anyway.

We might perhaps be persuaded to stand still for some time in the middle of our village square, but there weren't enough armed men to drag us all the way to town and put us in prison.

We knew these men in black shirts. They had come at night, otherwise they wouldn't have had the pluck. Most of them stank of wine, and if you looked them in the eyes they didn't like it and looked away. They were poor folk, too, but a special kind of poor folk; landless, not brought up to any trade, or knowing too many trades, which is the same thing. They were the type that dislike hard work, and live from one week to the next, from hand to mouth, always having to find new dodges to earn their daily bread. Too weak and servile to rebel against the authorities and the rich, they preferred cringing to them in return for the privilege of robbing and oppressing other poor folk – peasants and the poorer landowners and tenant-farmers. If you met them in the street in daytime they would be humble and fawning. By night and in numbers they were wicked and evil. They have always been at the disposal of anyone who gives orders, and they always will be. But recruiting them into a special army, giving them a special uniform and special arms, is something new and peculiar to the last few years.

Such are the so-called Fascists.

Their boldness had another explanation, too. Each of us would have been a match for at least three of them. But what chance had we in their midst? What was there to bind us together? What link was there between us?

There we all were in the middle of the square. We were all born at Fontamara. That was the only thing we had in common. Every one of us thought first of himself. Everyone tried to think of the best way of getting out of that square of armed men and leaving the others behind. Every one of us had a family, and we all thought of our families.

The only exception was possibly Berardo, but he had no land and no wife.

In the meantime other peasants had arrived from the Fucino, among them Ciammaruga's husband, and they were let into the square, too.

By this time it was very late.

The little fat man said:

'Let's begin the interrogation!'

Interrogation? What interrogation?

They made a kind of passage-way about a yard wide inside the square, and the fat man and Filippo Il Bello took up their stations one on each side of it.

The interrogation began. The first to be called was Teofilo the sacristan.

'Long live who?' the little fat man asked.

Teofilo came down to earth with a bump.

'Long live who?' repeated the representative of the law.

Teofilo turned his pathetic, terrified face towards us, in the hope of finding some inspiration, but we were as bewildered as he was.

As Teofilo gave no sign the man turned to Filippo Il Bello, who had a large book in his hand, and said to him:

'Put down "refractory".'

They let Teofilo go. The second to be called was Anacleto the tailor.

'Long live who?' the little fat man asked him.

Anacleto, who had had time to think, said:

'Long live Mary!'

'Which Mary?' Filippo Il Bello asked him.

'Mary of Loreto.'

'Write down "refractory",' the little man said.

They let Anacleto go. The next to be called was old Antonio Braciola. He had an answer ready, too.

'Long live San Rocco!' he cried.

But this answer wasn't satisfactory.

'Write down "refractory",' the little fat man said.

The fourth to be called was Pasquale Cipolla.

'Long live who?' he was asked.

'Excuse me, but what do you mean?' Cipolla dared to say.

'Answer clearly what is in your mind. Long live who?' the little fat man said.

'Long live bread and wine,' was Pasquale Cipolla's perfectly genuine answer. But he was put down as 'refractory,' too.

Each one of us was expecting his turn, and not one of us could guess what it was that the representative of the authorities wanted us to answer.

Our chief worry, of course, was whether there would be anything to pay if we gave the wrong answer. Nobody knew what 'refractory' meant, but we knew quite well what 'pay up' meant.

I tried to get as near as I could to General Baldissera, who was the best educated among us and had been to Naples in his youth, in the hope of picking up a hint about what to answer, but he looked at me with a superior, compassionate smile, as of one who knows the truth but knows it for himself alone.

When the little fat man asked him 'Long live who?' the old cobbler took his hat off and shouted:

'Long live Queen Margaret!'

The effect was other than what Baldissera expected. All the armed men roared with laughter, and the little fat man said:

'She's dead. Queen Margaret is dead.'

'She's dead?' the old cobbler exclaimed, horrified. 'Impossible!'

'Write down "constitutionalist",' the little fat man said.

Baldissera went away, shaking his head sadly after this sequence of inexplicable events. On Berardo's instructions

Antonio Zappa, whose turn came next, shouted: 'Down with the robbers!' This called forth a murmur of protest from the men in black shirts.

The little fat man ordered Filippo Il Bello to write down 'anarchist'.

Zappa went away, and it was Antonio Spaventa's turn.

'Down with the vagabonds!' he shouted. This caused a fresh outburst from the ranks of the blackshirts. Spaventa was put down as an anarchist as well.

'Long live who?' the little fat man asked Luigi Della Croce. But he was a pupil of Berardo's, too, and wouldn't shout 'long live' anything, but only the reverse.

'Down with the taxes!' was his reply.

This time the Fascists made no protest, but Della Croce was put down as an anarchist, too.

Raffaele Scarpone, who shouted 'Down with the people who pay the wages!' right in the face of the representative of the law, caused a much greater sensation.

The little fat man wanted to have him arrested, but Raffaele took the precaution of being well outside the square before he said the words. In two bounds he was behind the church, and that was the last we saw of him.

The next few were more prudent. The first of them was Giacobbe Losurdo.

'Long live everybody!' was his reply and it was hard to think of anything safer than that. But it wasn't appreciated.

'Put down "Liberal",' said the little fat man to Filippo Il Bello.

'Long live the Government!' shouted Giovanni Uliva, with the best of intentions.

'Which government?' asked Filippo Il Bello.

Uliva had never heard that there was more than one government, but out of politeness said: 'The lawful government!'

'Put down "traitor",' the little fat man said to Filippo Il Bello.

Ponzio Pilato tried to go one better, and when it was his turn shouted: 'Long live the Government!' too.

'Which government?' Filippo Il Bello asked.

'The unlawful government!'

'Put down "criminal",' the little fat man said.

Nobody had yet managed to find the right answer. As more and more wrong answers accumulated the choice of possible answers gradually became more and more restricted. But the really big point on which we were still absolutely in the dark was whether or not we would have to pay something as the result of giving the wrong answer. Berardo alone didn't seem to be worried by this possibility but amused himself by suggesting insolent answers to his young friends, on the basis of 'down with so-and-so' instead of 'long live so-and-so'.

'Down with the bank!' shouted Venerdì Santo.

'What bank?' asked Filippo Il Bello.

'There's only one and it only gives money to the Contractor,' said Venerdi, who was very well informed.

'Put down "Communist",' said the little fat man.

Gasparone was put down as a Communist, too, because his answer was 'Down with Torlonia!'

Palummo was put down as a Socialist for replying:

'Long live the poor!'

Meanwhile Maria Vincenza, Berardo's grandmother, arrived from the other side of the square. Just previously we had seen her going into Maria Grazia's house.

'Berardo! Where is Berardo?' the old woman was crying. 'What have these brigands done in our houses? What have they done to our women? And our men? Where are our men? Berardo!'

Berardo immediately understood, or pretended to understand. In one bound he was in front of Filippo Il Bello, who was livid with fear. He seized him by the collar and asked:

'Where is Elvira? What have you done to Elvira?'

Old Maria Vincenza had by this time arrived at the

96

threshold of the church, gone down on her knees, and begun to pray:

'Our Lady, protect us, save us, intercede for us!'

She was still praying when a stroke of the big church bell made us all look up to the top of the tower.

What we saw there was a ghost, a phantom of a woman, young, tall, thin, with a face as white as snow, leaning with her hands on the balustrade.

It took our breath away. Then the vision vanished.

'It's Our Lady! It's Our Lady!' shouted Filippo Il Bello, terror-stricken.

The other armed men began to shout: 'It's Our Lady! It's Our Lady!'

The square of armed men melted away in headlong flight to the lorries just outside the village.

We heard the engines being started up. Then we saw the lorries going down the hill at top speed, with headlights on. There were so many we couldn't count them. The procession seemed never-ending.

At the bottom of the hill, at the last bend in the road before it joins the high-road, we saw the procession of lorries suddenly stop. The stop lasted more than half an hour.

'What have they stopped for? Do you suppose they're coming back?' I asked Berardo.

'Raffaele Scarpone knows why they've stopped,' he answered, laughing.

By the time the lorries had started up again it was very late.

'Shall we go to bed or wait another hour or so and go to the Fucino?' I asked Berardo.

'The first thing to do is to see who's in the church tower,' said Berardo.

Berardo believed in the Devil, but not in Our Lady. If the Devil had appeared, he would have believed it, but he wouldn't believe it if it was Our Lady.

We climbed the tower and found my wife and Elvira

more dead than alive.

(Next day we learnt that the procession of lorries stopped at the bottom of the hill because the first lorry capsized. It had run straight into a tree trunk that had been placed across the road. There had been a number of injured, including the little fat man with the tricolour round his waist.)

6   That night's ordeal sent Elvira to bed.

Just previously she had received a little wool to weave and dye, and she was very upset at not being able to work. In our part of the country the art of weaving reached its lowest ebb during the War. Elvira's loom was one of the few still in use, but she had less and less to do. It was only rarely now that anyone had a few yards of wool for her to weave and dye. In neighbouring villages bonfires had been made of looms that had been worked for centuries. Many things had contributed to killing the trade – the disappearance of local flocks of sheep, the introduction of town-made woollen goods and the ever-increasing poverty of the peasants.

Elvira asked Berardo to help her by chopping wood for the fire, and Berardo willingly accepted, and wouldn't hear of taking any pay. He didn't only chop wood, but, under Elvira's guidance, started dyeing wool for her, too.

Elvira would remain in a corner, stretched on her straw pallet. She was still pale from the shock of that night, and perhaps the more beautiful because of her pallor, with her round, dark face, black eyes and hair, and slender figure. She would give orders, and Berardo would obey them, like a baby learning something new. Sometimes, too, he would ask questions that would perplex Elvira, as when he asked why a piece of yellow cloth would turn dark blue after being dipped in indigo.

'Why, it couldn't do anything else,' she would answer.

'But why?' asked Berardo.

'Because it just couldn't,' Elvira would say, and then to get her own back, she would ask:

'Why don't sunflower seeds grow up into onions?'

'Don't try to be funny,' Berardo would answer. 'It's quite obvious that if what I sow are really sunflower seeds they won't grow up into onions.'

This kind of question wasn't likely to lead to any harm. Every time I went to the dyeing shop to see if Elvira wanted anything I found Berardo busy round the two brick vats that filled up nearly half the room. The air was dense with vapour, and Berardo would move and lift the cloths boiling in the vats with a long, black pole, or else stoke the fire.

One night Elvira made another attempt, in my presence, to make Berardo accept a few lire in payment, but Berardo refused them in his usual abrupt way

'If Berardo won't take the money it's because he wants you to put it aside for the wedding-day,' I said.

Elvira got as red as a berry, and Berardo looked at me as if he wanted to hit me.

Oh, well, it can't be helped, I thought to myself. Berardo isn't a marrying man.

Next morning Maria Vincenza, Berardo's grandmother, came to see me.

'Have you seen Berardo?' she asked me.

'What?' I said astonished. 'Didn't he come home last night?'

'No, he didn't,' the old woman said, and went away.

A little later Berardo turned up. He stopped at the door without even saying good morning, and I let him be, without saying anything either. When I was ready to go down to the fields he said to me:

'I want some advice.'

It was the first time in his life that that man had ever asked anyone for advice.

'It's about marriage,' Berardo went on. 'Yesterday, when you hinted at it, it wasn't urgent, but now it is.'

Then I realised that Berardo had spent the night with Elvira.

'My advice is that you hurry up and marry Elvira. You've got everything to gain and nothing to lose,' I said. 'There isn't a better match in Fontamara.'

'You don't understand,' Berardo said to me. 'Have I ever hoped for a better woman than Elvira? Never. What am I? A landless peasant, a mole without a burrow, a fox without a hole. Even if Elvira is prepared to marry me as I am, without any land, it isn't good enough. If Elvira hasn't got sense, I have. There's no harm in starving by myself or with my grandmother. But am I to starve with Elvira in my house? There's no harm in going out day-labouring, first for one boss, then for another. But is Elvira's husband to go out day-labouring? Is Elvira's husband to be a landless peasant?'

'Why didn't you think of all that before?' I said to him. 'Why didn't you think of that last night, before you slept with Elvira?'

'You don't understand,' said Berardo, getting angry 'It's not as if I were willing to give Elvira up. It's not as if I were willing to let anyone else have her.'

That's how Berardo used to argue about everything. You could argue with him all day long without getting anywhere.

But this time the point at issue seemed perfectly simple, so to cut it short I asked him a perfectly straightforward question.

'Do you want to marry Elvira or don't you?'

'You haven't understood anything and you never will understand,' said Berardo, and off he went.

Berardo seemed very depressed. The root of all the trouble was the fact that he didn't own any land.

Up to now, with his usual far-fetched arguments, he had managed to evade the issue, but the immediate necessity of setting up a household brought him face to face with it.

Most of the peasants of Fontamara and the neighbouring villages are small proprietors or lessees of a strip of land. The number of peasants who don't possess any land at all is very small indeed. The landless peasant is despised and looked down on by everyone. He is frequently forced to change his job, and during the last few years his wages have been cut and cut. At one time, when land was cheap, the peasant-labourer was looked upon in all the villages as the laziest, most ignorant, most stupid and most backward of all, and, as a matter of fact, there were lots of them that seemed to justify this verdict. But things had changed in the last few years. Smallholders no longer increased their holdings and not a single labourer ever became a smallholder. On the contrary, I could quote many cases of smallholders being sold up by their creditors and reduced to the condition of labourers. Even rich farmers had been reduced to the condition of smallholder-peasants. Whatever you might say about Berardo Viola, you couldn't deny that he was superior to anyone in Fontamara, both in character and intelligence. If he couldn't manage to save the money to buy a piece of land, it meant that the times when labourers could become smallholders had gone by. Most of the young men of Fontamara were in the same position.

Although times had changed people still used to think in the same old way. The landless peasant was still looked down on. Berardo could not learn to accept his position. He had always hoped to realize his ambition by going to America, or to some other part of Italy, but he had never succeeded. Confronted with the prospect of immediate and inevitable marriage, he felt himself condemned for life to a status inferior to that of the other peasants. There was no way out.

We had unexpected news about what conditions of work in towns were like from someone we had never expected to see in Fontamara again.

A little, bent old man, who looked neither like a peasant nor a townsman, or rather like a peasant all dressed up as a townsman, arrived panting one night in the little square of Fontamara. He carried a bag on his shoulders, and we immediately took him for one of those rural prophets who go about forecasting the crops, distributing charms against disease, curing women and beasts of the evil eye and selling the one and only remedy for corns.

General Baldissera saw him pass in front of his shop, and followed him out of curiosity, and fetched Marietta Sorcanera, Michele Zompa, Berardo Viola and me. 'Where do you come from and what do you prophesy about?' he asked him.

The little old man went on to the middle of the square put down his bag, sat down on it as if he were too exhausted to remain on his feet another minute, and replied:

'No one is a prophet in his own country.'

We didn't grasp what he was driving at.

The little old man was very queer to look at. He had a small head, like a baby's, watery eyes, long, old-fashioned moustaches, and an enormous, bulbous nose like an eggplant. It looked as if wine of various vintages would come out of it if you pressed it. He had a hard, melon-shaped hat on the top of his head, and wore a coat with a velvet collar and two rows of shining buttons. His trousers were grey, like a soldier's.

'Tell somebody's fortune, or something, but don't ask for any money,' Michele said to him.

'Just wait a moment, please,' he said, 'but first of all go and fetch Giuditta Goriano.'

'She's dust and ashes,' Michele answered, meaning that Giuditta was dead. We all began to laugh, because the old man hadn't proved himself a very good prophet.

'If Giuditta's dead, go and fetch Berardo Goriano,' said the false prophet.

'Berardo Goriano's dead, too,' Sorcanera answered. 'He died before the War.'

'And Peppino Goriano, is he dead, too?' the prophet asked, this time losing his temper.

Opinions differed about Peppino Goriano. Sorcanera, who had had a love affair with Peppino Goriano in her youth, maintained that he had long since died in Rome. Baldissera believed that he had made his fortune in Rome and married a rich wife and must long ago have forgotten the name of his native village.

'Very well, then,' said the old man, 'I'll tell you the true story of Peppino Goriano.

'Peppino Goriano left Fontamara for Rome in the year in which King Humbert was assassinated. How many years ago was that? That's easy to work out. From the death of King Humbert to the comet that arrived after the war of Tripoli was about ten years. From the comet to the war of Trieste was five years. That makes fifteen. The war of Trieste lasted four or five years and that makes twenty. Then for five years the trades unions were in power, and that makes twenty-five, and then came the Age of Order, which has lasted ten years, and everyone's hoping it will come to an end because it couldn't be worse to be governed by the Turks, but the Age of Order isn't coming to an end and there's no sign of the Turks, and that makes thirty-five.

'Well, Peppino Goriano left for Rome thirty-five years ago to make his fortune, and he intended to return to Fontamara as soon as he had made it, to marry a girl of sixteen he was in love with and whose name was then Marietta Sorcettonero. . .'

'That was me,' said Sorcanera, blushing.

'Impossible!' said the prophet, looking Marietta up and down.

We spoke up for her, however, and the prophet was upset

and stopped telling his story in some confusion. After a pause, however, he went on.

'Peppino Goriano reckoned on making his fortune in a couple of years. He found work in Rome immediately, as a dish-washer at the Institute of Charitable Friars, but he didn't make his fortune. He worked fourteen hours a day and earned enough to eat and sleep, but not to drink. The priests of the Institute believed that wine was degrading to man, so they wouldn't allow their dependents to be degraded. The only people in the Institute who had the right to be degraded were the Fathers Superior. But the wine the Fathers Superior drank was kept in the cellar, and Peppino Goriano used to work in the cellar. So after two years of faithful service he was sacked for continual drunkenness. After that he was out of work for some time. He would earn a few ha'pence now and then, but not enough to satisfy his thirst, much less to let him sleep and eat. He would sleep in the Botanical Gardens or in the Colosseum, or beneath the porches of the Esedra, according to the time of year. One night Peppino Goriano dreamt that he saw a vision of San Rocco, who explained to him how to enter a neighbouring provision shop. Peppino immediately awoke and dashed to the provision shop, but he was caught by the police and sentenced to eight months' imprisonment. During the trial he tried to explain about San Rocco, but the judges wouldn't believe him. Judges as a rule don't believe people in misfortune.

'But in prison Peppino did make his fortune. He caught a disease of the eyes. First of all a whitish fluid started coming out of his eyes, then they became swollen, and then red, like small tomatoes. It was pitiable to behold. Thanks to the lamentable condition of his eyes, Peppino was released from prison and then, for the first time in his life, he managed to seize fortune by the forelock. He hired a baby girl from an acquaintance, and in the morning he would, as a rule, tour the churches in which Mass was being said for souls in Purgatory. At midday he would go and get a plate of soup from two or three convents; and in the afternoon he would take up advantageous positions outside cemeteries and entrances to theatres. Although the baby girl cost him two lire a day, Peppino managed to earn enough to pay for his lodgings and lay a little money aside. He had no need to worry about food, because he got only too much of it from the various convents, and he used to sell a portion of it to an inn at the Porta San Giovanni in exchange for wine. Peppino intended living on alms for at least a couple of years, in order to save enough money to return to Fontamara and marry Sorcettonero. . .'

'Why did he change his mind?' asked Marietta with a sigh.

'It was, as usual, envy that prevented him from carrying out his plans. A sad day came when a policeman took him to hospital to have his eyes cured. Peppino Goriano tried to object. "They're my eyes, and I can do what I like with them," he said. But there has never been real liberty in Italy. His eyes were cured in a few days, but he had lost his livelihood. The happy times, the times of plenty, were over, and a time of penitence began. He tried navvies' jobs, like bricklaying, carting and rowing boats on the Tiber, but he didn't stick to any of them longer than a week. When he had the will he hadn't the strength, and when he had the strength he hadn't the will. He tried to make his fortune in a thousand other ways.

'In those days hundreds of people came to Rome from the provinces, hoping to make their fortune. Those with small ambitions got jobs as crossing-sweepers, shoe-cleaners, kitchen-hands, gardeners or stable-lads, and managed to build up some sort of a modest position for themselves, laying aside a little money every day. But Peppino hadn't the patience to wait ten years to save a thousand lire like the other people from the country. He expected any day to find the open-sesame that would lead to fortune. Instead the gates of prison would quite frequently shut on him.

Altogether he spent four years and five months in prison.

'After all these failures Peppino Goriano began to lose heart. He got resigned to leading the life of the poor people from the Abruzzi who do all the more humble jobs in Rome. For some time he went about in the neighbourhood of the station and the barracks quarter with a parrot which in return for a penny would give you an envelope containing your fortune, but after a few months the parrot began to show signs of mental instability and died. Then Peppino started making something out of the people who continually streamed into Rome from the Abruzzi, wanting work for the winter months. He opened an employment agency, finding women situations as nurses and housemaids and men jobs as dish-washers and builders' labourers.

'About that time Peppino struck up an acquaintance with a reverend gentleman, Monsignor Calogero, a barefooted Carmelite, who took him into his service as steward. Monsignor suffered from concupiscence more than was decent at his age, and peasant girls from the Abruzzi were his favourite means of assuaging it. Peppino got free board and lodging, plus ten lire for every peasant girl he succeeded in introducing to the reverend gentleman's bed. For the first few months Peppino did his work conscientiously, and continually walked the avenues and public gardens trying to persuade servant girls to go and confess to Monsignor Calogero. The results were very meagre. Besides, the reverend gentleman would never have the same woman more than two or three times, and you had to be continually finding new ones. In order not to lose his job Peppino had to have recourse to the women of the Via Panico who make love professionally. He made them eat onions and garlic to encourage Monsignor Calogero in the belief that he was dealing with country girls just arrived from the Abruzzi. The reverend gentleman did not notice the deception until one day he caught a nasty disease. Peppino Goriano got the sack. Misfortune dogged him once more.'

'But why didn't he come back to Fontamara?' Marietta asked.

'Come back to Fontamara like a beggar? Out of the question. He stayed in Rome, where he found poverty more supportable. He did a thousand jobs; clipping dogs, bell-ringing, grave-digging, selling bootlaces in the street and postcards in memory of Guglielmo Oberdàn, dish-washing in various restaurants. The more he changed his jobs the more they were the same.

'Thousands of people from the Abruzzi lived and live in Rome as he did, doing what the "others" don't condescend to do. They pass their lives on a lower level than the "others". They remain poor peasants for life, as poor as church mice. You can spot them in the street on sight. On Sundays the "others" go to the stadium or the Parioli Gardens; they go to some wretched inn. Peppino was in Rome when the "others" were demonstrating for or against the war of Trieste; all he did was to go to a miserable little inn near the Porta Trionfale. After the war almost all the "others" would go to the trades unions; he would go to an inn at Testaccio. He never got embroiled with the "others" except when the whole city was in a turmoil, and then he didn't mean to. And he paid dearly for it.

'One day, for instance, Peppino Goriano was walking down the Via Cola da Rienzo when a large crowd with a red flag started raiding the shops. He mingled with the crowd, entered a boot shop, and when he was outside again realised that the two shoes he'd taken were odd ones. He had two lady's dancing-shoes, both for the left foot, and a large riding-boot for the right foot. What on earth was he to do with them? He tried to find who'd got the boots and shoes to match those he'd taken, and asked everybody he came across, until he met a very smart gentleman, who said that he would be happy to be of service to him and asked him to his house. He did not take him to his house, however, but to the police station, where he was arrested and accused of looting. When the case came up for trial Peppino appeared in the dock with a lot of other workmen, who all declared that their motive for taking part in the raid on the shops had been political. But Peppino admitted that he had been in need of boots, and was punished twice as heavily as the others.

'In those times if a man were killed in the street the murderer was actually acquitted and rewarded if he said he had done it for political reasons, but given a ferocious sentence if he'd done it because he was hard up. Peppino decided, after thinking the matter over, that the reason he had remained a nobody all his life was that he had done everything he had done because he was hungry and not for political reasons. Although not a youngster any more, he decided that whatever he did in the future would be done for political reasons.

'At the end of his sentence Peppino was summoned by the police and told to make his choice. "Either you do what we tell you or you leave Rome and return to Fontamara this very night," they said to him. Similar alternatives had been given to friends of his who had recently been released from Regina Coeli. Peppino wholeheartedly accepted the police proposal that he should do political work. He received an advance of fifty lire and was ordered to go to the Piazza Venezia that very night and shout "Long live Nitti! Down with Fiume!" '

'Do you mean to say he got fifty lire for doing nothing but shout?' Michele asked the false prophet, expressing our utter disbelief.

'Don't interrupt. You don't understand anything about politics. That night Peppino Goriano went to the Piazza Venezia, where he found a large crowd of people, among them a number of friends of his from Regina Coeli. He started shouting "Long live Nitti! Down with Fiume!" He saw a crowd of officers and soldiers advancing towards him, while his friends from Regina Coeli fled helter-skelter in all directions. But he was at the very beginning of his political career and wanted to keep his job, so he went on shouting what the police had told him to shout, without even knowing what it meant. Peppino was surrounded by the officers and men, and he has never been able to remember what happened next, because he lost consciousness and only came round in the hospital of San Giacomo.'

'You mean to say the officers were against the police? How could that be possible?' asked General Baldissera, who had a high opinion of military discipline.

'Don't interrupt,' said the false prophet. 'You don't know anything about politics. Peppino went on doing political work, that is to say, he went on taking thrashings at times and places determined by the police. He was thrashed till the blood ran by the tramway-workers at Porta Santa Croce, by the gas-workers at Porta San Paolo, by the foundry-workers at the Porta Trionfale. Wherever he went to shout what the police told him to shout he got a thrashing. Usually he was left to take the thrashing alone, because his colleagues from Regina Coeli fled as soon as things got nasty.'

'But why didn't Peppino run away, too?' asked Marietta, who was quite upset.

'To make more money,' the false prophet explained. 'The police paid him five lire a day, plus twenty-five lire consolation money whenever he was sent to hospital. In view of the cost of living five lire a day wasn't enough, so it was absolutely necessary for him to take thrashings. Naturally this wasn't very agreeable, but then work never has been agreeable. I may add that the words he had to shout were always being changed. After shouting "Long live Nitti!" for six months Peppino had to shout "Down with Nitti!" for a whole year. But the result was always the same; he always got beaten. After a year and a half of political activity Peppino Goriano's body was like that of Christ's after He was scourged, when Pontius Pilate said: "Behold, the man!"'

'Peppino Goriano could be regarded as a real political martyr. No Italian has ever suffered so much for the sake of politics. He wasn't one of those who stay at home and send others out to fight. He paid with his own body. Many other Italians fought for their ideals at that time, but not one of them could be compared to Peppino Goriano, who fought for all their ideals, who gave his blood for democracy, for Nationalism, for Socialism and for the Church. He found something good in each of them; in their service he earned five lire a day, plus twenty-five lire each time he went to hospital.

'But as he grew older Peppino found thrashings more and more difficult to bear. He began to be tormented with the ambition to retire from politics. Political strife was growing more and more dangerous. Demonstrators no longer used sticks and stones, they began to shoot. Politics started getting murderous. Politics ceased to be the art of earning a living by taking thrashings. Politics became grim and earnest, and entirely out of keeping with the character of Peppino Goriano.'

'But what did they want to shoot for?' Sorcanera asked.

'I've been in Rome thirty-five years and I haven't the slightest idea. How could an ignorant woman like you, who have spent the whole of your life at Fontamara, expect to understand?' replied the false prophet, somewhat evasively. Then he went on:

'It was all these politics. Peppino gave up answering the police summonses. After some time he was sent for and given the usual alternatives. "Either you do what we tell you or you leave Rome this very night and go back to Fontamara." But this time it wasn't a case of taking thrashings. It was a new kind of politics: twenty lire a day wages, a free pass on the trams, and the right to beat and not be beaten.'

'Don't talk nonsense!' Michele Zompa interrupted. 'Do you mean to say the police paid Peppino Goriano twenty lire a day, plus a free pass on the trams, for the right to beat people without the risk of being beaten in return? Don't talk rubbish. I have to work three whole days at the Fucino to earn twenty lire.'

The false prophet stopped, as if uncertain whether to go on. But after a while he went on, without taking any notice of Michele's interruption.

'This time it was a new and splendid kind of politics, a kind never known before. It was this so-called Fascism. What did Peppino Goriano think of Fascism? He thought it marvellous. Good pay, three times better than that of a poor peasant, and the right to give people beatings without being beaten in return, to say nothing of official protection.

'Peppino was taken by a policeman to a large hall behind the printing works of the *Giornale d'Italia*. When he got there, there was a large crowd of officers, students, clerks, smartly-dressed women, business men, and two or three priests, among them Monsignor Calogero. The walls were decorated with tricolour flags. Everybody was talking at the top of his voice. Peppino felt very frightened in the presence of so many distinguished people. But in a corner he found a group of people he knew, old friends from Regina Coeli, most of them housebreakers. Then there was an impressive silence. A gentleman went up on the platform and began to speak. He extended a hearty welcome to Peppino Goriano and his friends, "the new aristocracy of Labour", the most politically conscious section of the factory workers, ready to spill the last drop of their blood in the service of their country. Then the things that he went on to say became completely incomprehensible.

'After the speech was over the hall emptied and Peppino Goriano and his friends were invited to stay behind and take part in the conquest of Porta Pia.

'They were given food and drink in a neighbouring inn, and from there they were taken in a lorry to Porta Pia, near the La Breccia monument, where they waited for about an hour. From the place where they were waiting they saw troops of gendarmes and royal guards entering the offices of a

Communist newspaper and bringing out as prisoners all those who were inside. A policeman came to warn Peppino Goriano and his men that everything was now ready and that there was nothing to fear and that they could now safely storm the newspaper offices. They did so; the offices were raided; the furniture was brought into the middle of the street and burned, together with the books and papers. The windows, the doors, the typewriters, the pictures, the stoves were smashed into a thousand pieces, the bottles of ink were smashed against the walls, the safe was scientifically broken open, but it was empty.

'Before they left the wrecked offices, the raiders were photographed by a lot of journalists who turned up. Peppino was in the middle of the group, brandishing the leg of a table. Next day his photograph appeared in the Piccolo, with the caption "The Hero of Porta Pia".

'Peppino had a number of unforgettable days of glory and renown. He would hang round newspaper offices, at each of which he would be given money for drinks. He actually got an invitation from the Marchesa Parucchini, who introduced him to her friends, and then took him to her kitchen and then to her bedroom, where he had much more tiring work to do than at the conquest of Porta Pia.

'Peppino took advantage of his new-found glory to get a job as watchman at the night hostel of Borgo Pio. A friend of his was killed by the workers of the San Lorenzo district, and this gave him much food for thought. When he received more summonses from Fascist headquarters he answered that he was ill. He didn't earn much at his new job, but he didn't risk much either.'

'When the Fascists became bosses why didn't Peppino take advantage of it to get a better job?' Sorcanera wanted to know.

'When the Fascists became bosses, as you call it, bad times began for their old supporters. Peppino was summoned before a committee and asked: "Are you a Fascist? How long have you been a Fascist? Have you ever been in prison?" The consequence was the committee decided that criminals with several convictions for theft could not remain in the bosom of the Fascist Party, so Peppino Goriano, the Hero of Porta Pia, was expelled. The same thing happened to Peppino's friends whom the police had engaged on their release from Regina Coeli, with the exception of those who were still young and were accepted for the militia. At the same time Peppino was sacked from his job as watchman at the hostel of Borgo Pio, and was succeeded by a young man known as "the son of Monsignor Calogero".

'So a life of unemployment and hardship began again for Peppino. The old perpetual hunger, which he had never properly got rid of, came back. Every month life got more difficult. Nobody would ever have supposed that the new Government would last ten years, but it has lasted ten years.

'Rome has become impossible to live in. Every day there's a new law, every single day. True, every government always does make new laws, but this government makes a new law every single day.

'The Popes ruled for centuries with five laws only, with the five precepts of the Church. Garibaldi, after the Expedition of the Thousand, only introduced three new laws, the law of the knife, the law of the blood-feud and the law of drinking bouts. But the new Government has made laws about everything. There's a law forbidding you to talk of certain things, a law forbidding you to piss on the walls, a law forbidding you to walk on the left, a law forbidding you to sing at night or enter a tram by the front step. There's a law for those who won't get married, another law governing every possible kind of employment, another governing employment agencies, and another governing disputes between employers and employed.

'The more laws there are the more poverty there is. The more poverty there is the more laws they make. Rome is absolutely impossible to live in. The air stinks. The air of

114

Rome stinks.

'They've made lots of attempts to do away with it, but every time they've failed. Somebody said: perhaps the stink comes from the mice; so the municipality declared war on the mice and distributed poison to kill them off, and thousands and thousands of mice were destroyed. But the stink remained. Then somebody else said: perhaps the stink comes from the flies; so the municipality declared war on flies, and distributed liquids and powders to destroy the flies, and I don't know how many millions of flies were destroyed. But the stink remained. At certain times of the day it's strong enough to make you sick.'

'What does it come from? From the filth?' Michele asked.

'No one has ever found out what it comes from,' the prophet replied. 'It's least strong in the popular districts, Trastevere, San Lorenzo, Testaccio, more noticeable in the Prati, the clerks' quarter, but still bearable, but unwholesome and foul in the middle of the city, the ministers' quarter, and around St. Peter's. What does it come from? Nobody has the slightest idea. Some say it comes from the antiquity of Rome. An eternal city can't help being a stinking city. Some say it comes from corpses hidden in the underground passages of the public offices and the police station. Some even say it comes from all the stuff the new Government dragged out of the museums to make uniforms for ministers and ambassadors and porters – clothes, plumes, helmets, breastplates. Some people even say that the sewers are stopped up. There are plenty of other theories about, but the one thing that is quite definite is that the stink is still there and gets worse every day.

'Every week the police discover a new plot. Whole working-class districts get raided at night by thousands of armed men. Houses are searched from cellar to ceiling and hundreds are taken away under arrest. Nobody knows why. Everybody realises that one day his turn may come. Many live in a state of continual fear.

115

'Fear at Rome is like a disease, an epidemic. There are whole weeks and days of wholesale panic. It's enough to stare at anyone hard in the street or in an inn to see him grow pale and go away in a hurry. Why? Because of fear.'

'Fear of what?' Berardo asked.

'Just fear.'

'But fear of what?' Berardo asked.

'Just fear. No one knows why. Just fear. When fear grips a whole population there isn't any explanation. Fear grips everyone. It isn't only the opponents of the Government; the so-called Fascists are more frightened than anyone else. Even they say that things can't go on like this, and are afraid. Why do they murder their opponents? Because they're afraid. Why do they constantly increase the number of police and militia? Because they're afraid. Why do they put thousands and thousands of innocent people in gaol? Because they're afraid. The more crimes they commit the more frightened they get. The more frightened they get the more crimes they commit. Which leads to more fear and more crimes.'

'Is the Government strong?' Michele wanted to know.

'Its fear is very strong,' the prophet answered.

'And the Pope, what does he do?' Marietta asked.

'The Pope is frightened too. He accepted two thousand million lire from the new Government, bought a motor-car, installed a wireless, built a railway station for himself, although he never travels, installed a lot of other luxuries, and now he's got them he's getting frightened. The churches and convents of Rome got a letter from the Pope telling them to increase the amount of soup they give away to the poor. The soup is fear soup. They've added a bit of meat to the soup they give away on Thursdays at the Institute of the Charitable Friars. It's fear meat. There will have to be a lot of meat and soup before those two thousand millions are forgotten.'

'And how do the people from the provinces get on in Rome?'

'The rich people from the Abruzzi are doing well and the poor are doing badly, but they're all frightened. The police have begun a campaign of inquiry among the poor folk. An inquiry based on fear. Every week the police take a hundred of them and send them back to their native villages. Some of them have lived in Rome for thirty or forty years, and their native villages were destroyed in the 1915 earthquake, and not one of their relatives is still alive. But the police took them and sent them back "for reasons of public order". They took Peppino Goriano, gave him compulsory travelling papers, put him on the train and forced him to return to Fontamara, which he left thirty-five years ago. Well, he has returned.'

'Are you Peppino Goriano?' Marietta asked anxiously.

'Are you the Hero of Porta Pia?' asked General Baldissera.

He was.

7   The Hero of Porta Pia, having no home or relations of his own, took refuge in Marietta Sorcanera's marriage bed.

He seemed, in fact, to be ending up where he would have begun had the mirage of making his fortune in the city not led him astray since boyhood. But unlike Marietta, who was like a wolf that has lost its skin, but not its vice, and could always make a fresh start, the Hero as a man was unfortunately played out.

He would stay in the sun for hours, as still as a lizard.

'Why were we born?' he would ask if anyone went near him.

We didn't know what to answer. Who on earth knows why we were born?

Even General Baldissera no longer pretended to know. The amazing things we had learnt about the city had disturbed him more than anyone else. The old world in which he had stubbornly persisted in believing had been dead for thirty years, and a strange, fantastic world, in which incredible things happened, had taken its place.

Peasants still ploughed the land with wooden ploughs while townspeople darted across the sky in aeroplanes. Peasants had gone on saving coppers, twenty to the lire, while townspeople only talked in terms of thousand-lira notes. Peasants still went hungry, though they tilled the soil from dawn to sunset, while in town you could make a rapid fortune by beating people up in the streets.

Outside Fontamara no one now remembered the Christian general who had volunteered to go to Africa. No one now sang the old song:

Beware of the blacks . . .

The new Government in the city and its newspapers glorified the ridiculous figureheads who 'led' punitive expeditions against popular cafés, newspaper offices and private houses.

'What do they sing in town now?' General Baldissera asked the Hero of Porta Pia one day. You could tell from his voice the enormous importance he attached to the question.

The Hero got to his feet in the middle of the village square, and began to sing the latest popular novelty at the top of his voice:

Rend me,
Take my heart,
and rend me!. . .

At the station in Rome the Hero had been given a book containing Government propaganda addressed to the peasants. We expected to find in it some explanation of the Government's attitude to us, and one day we gathered round the Hero and asked him to read it.

The first part was dedicated to the reapers, and contained a poem. I copied it out, and have always carried it about with me, hoping that some day I might meet someone who could explain it to me. This is the poem:

Upon the hill-side, underneath the dome
  Of the unending sky, kissed by the sun
  The ploughman ploughs his furrows, one by one,

Cheered by the thought of happy harvest home.
While in the dull, oppressive plain below
    Borne by the breeze, sweet Alpine odours bring
    Relief, and lonely mountain-huts that cling
To ice-capped peaks, sweet peace, cool shadows know.

Like flocks of sheep, resting at sultry noon,
    The peasants' cottages, deep in the vale,
Lie sleeping; from afar is heard the boon
    Breaking the stillness, borne o'er hill and dale
And leafy glade – the gentle, murmuring tune
    Of falling waters; such bliss cannot fail.

Other passages in the book were clearer, and told of the blessed life of the fields. Among the arguments it contained I remember these:

When the townsman wants fresh air and repose, where does he go?

To the country!

Whence come fresh butter, pure oil, white flour, delicious fruit?

From the country!

The inhabitants of cities are thin, nervy, pale, depressed.

The inhabitants of the country are sturdy, happy, rosy-cheeked, and full of cheer.

What the new Government had done for the peasants was explained as follows:

Thanks to the new Government peasants do not now work more than eight hours a day.

Peasants are insured against accidents, illness and unemployment.

The taxes that the peasants used to pay have been reduced.

The banks are at the disposal of the peasants for raising credit.

When the Hero read out this passage we looked at one another, as if to say, he's trying to pull our leg.

The Hero passed the book to Michele Zompa, who read out the same thing. Michele Zompa passed it to Ponzio Pilato, who read it too, and he passed it to me and I read it myself.

Thanks to the new Government peasants do not now work more than eight hours a day.

Peasants are insured against accidents, illness and unemployment.

The taxes that the peasants used to pay have been reduced.

The banks are at the disposal of the peasants for raising credit.

At the end of the book it said:

In conclusion, power is in the peasants' hands. Italy is an agricultural country and its Government consists primarily of agriculturalists. The interests of the peasants are paramount. The peasants represent the country.

Michele expressed a suspicion that we all shared.

'This book must have been written by an enemy of the Government to make it a laughing-stock, or else it must have been written in a lunatic asylum.'

'That may be,' said the Hero, 'but it was given to me by the gendarmes.'

'What do the gendarmes want to distribute books like that for?' Berardo wanted to know. 'What does the Government of Prince Torlonia and the bank want to distribute books like that for? Why does it want to murder and rob the peasants in the peasants' name?'

We had learnt for the first time that this Government which had reduced the peasants to starvation had done so in the peasants' name.

'The Government has always been against the poor,' the Hero of Porta Pia tried to explain. 'But this Government is a special kind of government. It's against the poor, but in a special way. It exerts all its strength against the poor, but in a special way. There were many poor men among those who spilled their blood for the present Government. I don't mean myself and people like me, although no one could say we were rich. I mean clerks and tramway-men and railway-men and bricklayers, who were among the first Fascists. I mean those who are in the Fascist militia now. Most of them are not millionaires but poor peasants. Without them the present Government couldn't stay in power for long. The present Government needs them. The Government of Prince Torlonia and the bank needs them. The more the Government does for Prince Torlonia and the banks, the more it needs them, and the more necessary it is to have it believed that it is the Government of the peasants and all the workers.'

What the Hero of Porta Pia meant wasn't very clear to us. But then for some time nothing whatever had been clear to us.

What was quite clear was that the militia had come to Fontamara and raped a number of women. But they had done so in the name of the law and in the presence of a police commissary, and that was not so clear.

At the Fucino they had put up the rents of the smallholders and lowered the rents of the rich tenants. That was clear. But the proposal to do this had been made by the representative of the poor peasants, and that was not so clear.

On various occasions the so-called Fascists had beaten, wounded and even killed people against whom the law had no complaint, whose only crime was that they had been a nuisance to the Contractor, and that was perfectly clear. But those who had done these things had always been rewarded by the authorities, and that was not so clear.

Each one of our misfortunes, examined separately, was not new, for similar misfortunes had often happened in the past. But the way they befell us was new and strange.

The whole thing was absolutely beyond our understanding.

The small quantity of Fontamara-grown corn that the harvest now in progress would yield had been bought up by the Contractor back in May, when it was still green, for 120 lire a hundredweight. We had been very surprised that the Contractor, who was usually so cautious, should buy up corn in the middle of May, when no one could foresee its market price, but we needed the money and sold him the corn while it was still green, and the peasants of the neighbouring villages had done the same. The mystery was explained when reaping-time came. The Government made a special law concerning the national corn crop, and the price of corn jumped from 120 to 170 lire in consequence. Obviously the Contractor had heard about the law as early as May, so he made a profit of fifty lire on each hundredweight of our corn before it was even reaped.

Thus the whole of the profit from the growing of our corn went to the Contractor. The whole profit of the ploughing, the sowing, the harrowing, the weeding, the reaping, the threshing – the whole profit of a year's work had gone to the Contractor. The peasants ploughed the land and levelled it and sowed and dug and reaped and threshed, and when it was all done the Contractor came in and took the profits. The bank came in and took the profits.

Could we protest? We could not. The whole thing was legal, perfectly legal. The only thing that would have been illegal would have been for us to make a protest.

For a long time all the robberies committed against the peasants had been legal. If the old laws didn't suffice they made a new one.

Don Circostanza owed Berardo, Raffaele Scarpone and myself some money for replanting the vines in his old vineyard behind the cemetery, that had been ruined by a flood the year before. One Sunday morning we went to the house of the People's Friend to get it.

Don Circostanza shook us by the hand and embraced all

three of us, although he was sober.

'How many days' work do I owe you?' he asked.

He owed fifteen days' work to Berardo and twelve each to Raffaele Scarpone and myself.

It wasn't a very difficult sum to work out for an educated man like Don Circostanza.

But the face of the People's Friend darkened. He remained perfectly silent for several minutes. He paced two or three times up and down his study. He looked out of the window and listened at the keyhole to make sure he wasn't being overheard. Then he came up to us, scarcely able to control his feelings and said:

'It is terrible. You cannot imagine how we are being persecuted by the Government. Every day the Government imposes a new law on us. We are not even free any more to deal with our own money.'

This made a great impression on us. So the Government was actually beginning to persecute the gentlefolk, too.

'You have only to say the word, sir, and all the peasants will revolt,' said Berardo.

'No, no, no, there's no question of that!' said Don Circostanza terrified. 'It's something far worse. Look, there are the three envelopes I'd got ready for you; one for each of you, with the wages agreed upon.'

There were the three envelopes lying on the table.

'I prepared each envelope in accordance with the wages we agreed upon. I didn't hold a penny back. Do you believe me?'

'We believe you,' all three of us said.

He shook hands with us again, and embraced us. (Why shouldn't we believe him? If we couldn't trust him, whom could we trust?)

'Well,' the People's Friend continued, 'I received this morning the terms of the new labour contract for the agricultural workers of our province. It was a terrible and unexpected blow. Read it.'

I took the newspaper that Don Circostanza held out to me and read a few passages marked with a red pencil.

The current wage for agricultural workers is reduced by 40 per cent for workers of the first grade (men between nineteen and sixty years of age).

The wages of boys of seventeen and eighteen years of age (second grade) will be reduced by 20 per cent, in addition to the above reduction, and those of women and children (third grade) by 45 per cent.

'Isn't it terrible?' Don Circostanza said to us. 'Tell me, isn't it terrible?'

I read on:

All works of improvement to land or property planting or replanting vineyards, olive trees and fruit trees, the making of manure-heaps, filling up, clearing, excavating, digging ditches, road-making, etc., come into the category of public works in relief of unemployment and, as such, are to be paid at a rate lower than the above, the difference not to exceed 25 per cent.

'Isn't it absolutely intolerable?' said the People's Friend. 'What has the law got to do with the relations between employer and employed? What will become of our liberty if this goes on?'

'There are our three envelopes,' said Berardo. 'Let's take them, and that will be settled.'

Berardo made as if to pick up his own envelope, but Don Circostanza prevented him.

'What?' he cried, changing his voice and manner. 'Is that how you behave to me in my own house? In my very own house?'

'Why shouldn't he take it? It's his envelope!' I said. 'We worked for a fixed wage and for a fixed number of days. It isn't difficult to work out how much you owe us.'

'And the law – what about the law?' exclaimed the

People's Friend. 'Do you know what the penalty is for transgressing the law? You don't know anything about it, but I do. I don't intend to go to prison on your account. I'm very sorry indeed, but I regret that I absolutely cannot and will not go to prison on your account. The law is the law and must be respected.'

'The law of Moses says: "Thou shalt not steal",' I said.

'We're not concerned now with Moses, but with Mussolini,' said Don Circostanza. 'In any case, it isn't my business to preserve respect for the law. If you're not satisfied I'll send for the gendarmes.'

Don Circostanza was very upset. He strode up and down his study, his eyes blazing with anger.

'I should never have expected behaviour like this from you,' he said. 'After all I've done for you. All my life I've made sacrifices for the people. What do you mean by it? Do you want to ruin me? Why do you want to ruin me? Tell me frankly, why do you want to ruin me?'

Then he calmed down a little. He went to his writing-table. He picked up Berardo's envelope and took out eighty-five lire. Then he took a piece of paper and a pencil and began to reckon.

'According to the law,' he said, 'we must first of all deduct 40 per cent. 40 per cent is thirty-five lire. That leaves fifty-one lire. From that we must deduct 25 per cent in accordance with the law for the relief of unemployment. That is thirteen lire. Thirty-eight lire are left for Berardo. My dear Berardo, you're a very good fellow, and I am very sorry indeed, but you must blame it on the Fascists.'

Then Don Circostanza took my envelope, took seventy-eight lire from it, and started reckoning all over again.

'Let us first, in accordance with the law, deduct 40 per cent. That makes thirty-five lire. That leaves about forty-eight lire. Now deduct 25 per cent for unemployment relief. That makes twelve lire. Thirty-four lire are left for you.'

The same calculations were repeated for the benefit of

Scarpone.

Then, in a burst of generosity, Don Circostanza called his housemaid and offered us a glass of wine. There was nothing else for it. We drank it.

That same morning Baldovino Sciarappa and his wife had been sent for to see Donna Zizzola. Baldovino rented a piece of land from Don Carlo Magna, and had paid the rent just a few days before. Donna Zizzola had found the payment short, because the year before Baldovino's wife had brought her a present of two dozen eggs in addition to the rent. Donna Zizzola claimed that in accordance with the law of custom she should be brought the two dozen eggs every year in addition to the rent.

We found Baldovino Sciarappa beating his wife in the middle of the street just outside the People's Friend's front door. They had been to see Donna Zizzola, and had been forced to agree that the law of custom required them to bring her two dozen eggs every year in addition to the rent.

The idea of giving Donna Zizzola a present of two dozen eggs had been Baldovino's, but it had been his wife who had taken the eggs, and she hadn't explained that they were a single, special gift, not to be repeated. In other words the whole thing was his wife's fault. So this year and next year and in all future years, in fact for the whole of Baldovino's life, and after him for the whole of his son's life, Donna Zizzola would have the right, in accordance with the law of custom, to claim two dozen eggs in addition to the rent for that wretched little piece of land.

One thing was perfectly clear. Every day new laws were being made in favour of the landlords and the only old laws that were being abolished were those that favoured the peasants. The others remained.

Thus the law of custom, when it was a good custom, such as that of paying a peasant his stipulated wage, had been done away with, while the law of custom, when it was a bad custom, such as making a gift 'compulsory,' remained in force.

Donna Zizzola, in accordance with an old custom, like the other old-fashioned landowners, had a ring to measure the size of the eggs her tenants brought her as gifts. She would systematically refuse eggs that were small enough to pass through the ring. Now the ring dated back to a time when hens laid much bigger eggs than they do now, and Donna Zizzola would more and more frequently refuse small eggs and demand bigger ones instead. But was it the peasants' fault that the hens no longer laid eggs as big as before?

About that time Teofilo the sacristan had made a collection for Don Abbacchio to come and say a Mass for the people of Fontamara. The collection raised about ten lire, but Don Abbacchio answered that the price of Masses had gone up, and that he wouldn't come unless we sent him another ten lire. The other ten lire were collected with great difficulty, one copper at a time, and one Sunday morning Don Abbacchio came to say Mass.

The church was in a terrible state, full of dust and cobwebs with the walls peeling from damp in many places.

The only thing that was beautiful was the picture of the Eucharist on the altar. Jesus held a piece of white bread in His hand. He was saying:

'This is My body.'

In other words, white bread is My body. White bread is the Son of God. White bread is truth and life. Jesus wasn't referring to the maize bread that the peasants eat, nor to the tasteless and barren substitute for bread that is the consecrated wafer of the priests. Jesus had in His hand a real piece of white bread, and He was saying: 'This (the white bread) is My body.'

He meant the body of the Son of God, which is truth and life. He meant 'He who has white bread has Me (God).' He who lacks white bread, he who has only bread made of maize, is outside the grace of God, does not know God, does not know the truth, has no life. For him who has no white bread, for him who has only maize bread, it is as if Christ had never been, as if the Redemption were still to come.

How could we fail to think of our wheat, cultivated with so much labour all the year long, and then seized by the bank in the month of May when it was still green? We had cultivated it in the sweat of our brow, but we were not to eat of it. It was to go to town, where everyone would eat of it, even dogs and cats, but we were not to eat of it. We were to eat bread made of maize.

Christ, saying from the altar: 'This is My body,' was not pointing to a piece of maize bread, but to a piece of white bread. And the words of Our Father, 'Give us this day our daily bread,' did not mean bread made of maize, but bread made of wheat.

The bread that Jesus miraculously multiplied, together with the fishes, to still the hunger of the peasants of His country, was not bread made of maize but bread made of wheat.

The bread of the verse of the sacrament:

O living bread of Heaven

is not bread made of maize, but bread made of wheat (wheat that grows in the country, but is consumed in the town).

When Don Abbacchio came to the reading of the Gospel he turned to us and preached us a little sermon about San Berardo.

San Berardo was a peasant, and he has always been the peasants' saint. The most important miracle he performed during his lifetime was a great distribution of bread to the peasants of Pescina in a year of famine. He is therefore, in a sense, the saint of white bread, bread made of wheat.

San Berardo died in old age, after a life of great privation. It is said that when he died and appeared before the Judgment Seat, the Almighty, Who knew him and wished him well, embraced him and said:

'Everything you want is yours. Do not hesitate to ask whatever you wish.'

San Berardo was very much disturbed at this offer.

'Can I ask for *anything*?' he asked timidly.

'Whatever you like,' said the Almighty encouragingly. 'I give the orders here in Heaven. I can do whatever I like here. There's no Pope here. Besides, I wish you well. Whatever you ask is yours.'

But San Berardo didn't dare say what he wanted. He feared that his immoderate wishes might incur the wrath of God. Only after much persuasion on the part of God, and after He had given him His word of honour that He would not be angry, did San Berardo express his wish.

'O Lord,' he said, 'give me a large piece of white bread. '

God kept His word and did not get angry, but embraced the peasant-saint and wept with him. Then, in His voice of thunder, He summoned twelve angels and ordered them to provide San Berardo with the best white bread in Paradise *per omnia saecula saeculorum.*

That happened about four hundred years ago. Since then no peasant has gone to Paradise.

That is the true story of San Berardo, as handed down from father to son in our part of the country. The priests, however, tell it differently. According to the modern priests, no eating takes place in Paradise. In Paradise you enjoy the vision of God without eating. If that is true, it seems to be an additional reason for eating on this earth. Don Abbacchio apparently thought so too, for we knew him as a formidable glutton, one who tried to get fatter than he could possibly manage, in anticipation of an eternal fast.

Don Abbacchio finished his sermon by suggesting to us the idea of special nine days' devotions in order to obtain the protection of the Almighty for the population of Fontamara.

'A Mass is a fine thing, but it does not suffice,' he said. 'A Mass lasts half an hour and is then over. Which of you, if he has an important case to discuss with a lawyer, is satisfied to talk it over with him once only? The same persistence is necessary in the case of God. God is, of course, benevolent, but He likes to hear Himself being prayed to. For the special devotions it is necessary that a priest should stay in Fontamara for nine days, at the expense of the people. It would cost altogether about fifty lire. . .'

'Pay, pay, always pay,' Berardo audibly interrupted, and walked out of church. All the other men filed out behind him.

Don Abbacchio began the psalm and hurriedly finished the Mass, took off his chasuble and surplice and made his exit from the sacristy, his tail between his legs.

In good years priests do well. They say Mass, celebrate three days' special devotions and nine days' special devotions, take Holy Communion, give extreme unction, conduct funerals, and, if it's a good year, it's all right. But when famine is in the land what can a poor priest do?

At such times the peasants have always had only one relief – wrangling with each other.

Hardly two families at Fontamara were still on speaking terms. The slightest excuse was enough to cause the most violent quarrels. Quarrels would break out during the day between the women, and would burst out again in the evening when the men came home from work. They would be about a little bit of yeast which was borrowed and not returned, or about a brick or a barrel or a plate or a piece of wood or a chicken or a bit of straw.

When there's want, things to quarrel about turn up a dozen times a day. But the thing of all things to quarrel about was the water of the stream.

The road-menders quickly dug the new trench. On the day of the division of the waters all the peasants of Fontamara who had fields to irrigate turned out to watch.

A dam with two sluices had been built at the spot where the water was to be divided, to regulate the amount of water that was to flow along the old course and the amount that was to go to the Contractor. We were still puzzled about how it was going to be divided into that mysterious three-quarters each.

About a hundred gendarmes came from the town and were drawn up on the road. A squad came up to us and made us move away from the stream towards the vineyards. We let them, because we had never seen so many gendarmes before.

A little later a squad of Fascist militia and the guests of honour turned up, including the Contractor, the notary, Don Circostanza, the Thinker, Don Cuccavascio, Don Ciccone, Don Pomponio, Don Tarandella, the Hon. Pelino, in a black shirt, and a lot of other gentlemen whom we didn't recognize, and, last of all, Filippo Il Bello and Innocenzo La Legge.

Don Circostanza came straight towards us, shook hands with each of us, and told us to leave everything to him, for our own good. It was arranged that we should appoint a committee of elders to witness the division of the water. Ponzio Pilato, Giacobbe Losurdo and I were put on the committee. The other peasants were given permission to gather on the high-road, behind a cordon of gendarmes.

When all was ready the notary came towards us and read out the agreement between the people of Fontamara and the Contractor for the division of the stream.

'The agreement is perfectly clear,' said the notary. 'Three-quarters of the water is to flow along the new bed made by the commune and three-quarters of the remainder is to continue to flow along the old bed.'

'That's wrong!' Ponzio Pilato shouted. 'The agreement says three-quarters each, that means half each, that means three-quarters to us and three-quarters to the Contractor. Every man his fair share!'

'No, no, no!' Giacobbe Losurdo started shouting, too. 'The agreement says we are to have three-quarters of the water, and if there's any over it's to go to the Contractor – that is, if there is any over, because there's very little water anyway.'

'Three-quarters each is absolute rubbish,' I said. 'I've never heard of such a thing in all my life! The truth is that the water belongs to Fontamara and ought to go on belonging to Fontamara.'

The peasants who were gathered on the road, surrounded by a cordon of gendarmes, realised from our shouts and gestures that the division of the water was going against us, and raised an uproar. Raffaele Scarpone in particular started shrieking like a lost soul, seconded by his usual gang of wild youths.

'Since the inhabitants of Fontamara have adopted a provocative attitude and the members of the committee of elders appointed to be present at the division of the waters are not even in agreement among themselves, I avail myself of my powers as head of the commune, and appoint the Hon. Pelino, commander of militia, and Don Circostanza, to act as the representatives of Fontamara,' announced the Contractor.

Six gendarmes came up to us and led us to where the other people of Fontamara were standing on the high-road, while Don Circostanza shouted to us:

'Keep calm! keep calm! Put your trust in me!'

From behind the cordon of gendarmes we could hardly make out what was happening near the stream.

Secretly that did not altogether displease us, because it rid us of all responsibility towards the other inhabitants of Fontamara. It was better that our interests should be protected by an educated man like Don Circostanza.

First the notary, then an architect, then four road-menders with shovels approached the stream. The Hon. Pelino and Don Circostanza each had several consultations with the architect.

The high bank of the road and the large crowd of gendarmes and officials round the two sluices that were to regulate the division of the waters prevented us from seeing how the famous 'three-quarters each' was being interpreted. But, about a hundred yards lower down, the stream-bed formed a bend round Giacinto Barletta's and Papasisto's gardens, and there we would be able to see how much the flow of our water was going to be diminished and how much was going to remain. All our eyes were therefore fixed on that spot. We gazed and gazed at it and tried to guess what the officials and our own representatives were doing a few yards away.

Raffaele was the first to see the water-level sink. Not one of us had believed that we should be left as much water as we had before, but when we actually saw it sinking we all began to shout and curse at the Contractor and his guests.

'Thieves, thieves, thieves!' we shouted.

Filomena Quaterna, Recchiuta, Cannarozzo's daughter, Giuditta Scarpone, Lisabetta Limona and a number of other women went down on their knees and began the litany of curses:

'May they lose as much blood as they are stealing water from us!

'May they shed as many tears as they are stealing water from us!

'May toads be born in their bellies! May sea serpents be born in their bellies!

'May none of them ever see their wives and children again!

'Jesus, Joseph, St. Anne and Mary,

'Do me this grace for my soul!'

Meanwhile the water-level sank lower still, until we could see the stones, tufts and weeds that lined the bottom.

'*Consummatum est!*' we heard Don Abbacchio say.

'All our water! All our water! They've taken all our water!' we started shouting again. Raffaele Scarpone and Venerdì Santo, backed by other young men, hurled themselves against the cordon of gendarmes who were confining us to the main road. The gendarmes defended themselves with their rifle-butts and struck out wildly, shouting: 'Get back! get back!'

Don Circostanza managed with a great effort to make his voice heard above the uproar.

'Keep calm! keep calm!' he shouted. 'I'm here to defend your interests. Don't act recklessly; leave it all to me!'

Don Circostanza came towards us along the bank of the road and started one of his usual speeches.

'Have you lost confidence in me? That's why things are going badly with you, because you've lost confidence in me. Do you think you will gain anything by shouting and violence?'

Then he turned to the Contractor and said:

'The dissatisfaction of these people is justified. A compromise must be found. I appeal to your sense of humanity, I appeal to you as a friend of the people. The good people of Fontamara deserve to be respected. The commune has borne the expense of digging the new bed for the stream. What is done is done. It is one of the sayings of Christ, *quod factum est factum est. . .* '

'Quite right,' interrupted Don Abbacchio.

'I therefore propose that a term be established after which the stream must be returned in its entirety to the people of Fontamara. That should console the people of Fontamara. Their loss is legal, but not eternal! Let someone propose a term.'

'Fifty years!' the Contractor proposed.

A howl of indignation from us greeted this outrageous proposal.

'We'd rather have our throats cut! We'd all rather go to prison! Thief, thief!'

Don Circostanza managed to re-establish silence. He turned to the Contractor and said:

'In the name of the people of Fontamara I declare that I cannot accept the proposal of the *podestà*. Fifty years is too long. We must fix on a term far, far shorter than that.'

'Forty years,' proposed Don Abbacchio.

'Thirty-five,' proposed the Hon. Pelino.

'Twenty-five,' proposed the notary.

But every new proposal was howled down by the whole mass of peasants.

Don Circostanza came forward again.

'Permit me to make another proposal in the name of the good and industrious people of Fontamara. I propose a term of ten lustres. I appeal to the *podestà* in his kindness of heart to accept this great sacrifice!'

Don Tarandella, Don Ciccone, Don Pomponio, Don Cuccavascio and the Thinker all gathered round the Contractor to implore him to make this sacrifice on our behalf.

After a lot of persuasion the Contractor gave in.

A sheet of paper was produced, and the notary wrote out the form of words suggested by Don Circostanza and had it signed by the Contractor and by the Hon. Pelino and the author of the proposal himself as representing the people of Fontamara.

(As a matter of fact, not one of us had any idea how long ten lustres were.)

8   There was a lot of argument at Fontamara about how long ten lustres could possibly be.

The Hero of Porta Pia thought ten lustres were a hundred years, but General Baldissera maintained they were ten centuries.

Marietta Sorcanera tried to get her word in too. 'Couldn't it be ten months?' she said, but nobody listened to her.

In any case ten lustres meant hunger for Fontamara. Every day the gardens and fields at the bottom of the hill, which were formerly watered by the stream, looked more desolate. To make matters worse, as if the Almighty were in league with the Contractor, it hadn't rained since May.

Don Abbacchio took advantage of this to renew his proposal for special devotions, but Teofilo, the sacristan, was the first to object to the proposal, in words that were blasphemous for a churchman like him.

Down on the plain the whole crop was slowly being burned up. Large fissures made their appearance in the dry and parching soil. Viewed from a distance the maize fields of Ponzio Pilato and Antonio Ranocchia alone appeared to be exceptions – but only appeared. The stalks of the maize had grown tall, but the ears were rare and small, with tiny, meagre grains. At best they would only make forage for the beasts.

The plight of the fields belonging to Michele Zompa, Baldovino Sciarappa and me, which were sown with beans, was still worse. The beans looked like weeds burnt up by the sun. A torrent of molten lava might have passed over the fields of Giacinto Barletta, Venerdì Santo, Antonio Braciola and Papasisto.

It meant hunger for Fontamara.

Normally the produce of the soil we owned or rented just sufficed to pay our rents and taxes, while the produce of the irrigated fields furnished our food for the winter months – bread made of maize and vegetables for soups. The theft of our water condemned us to a winter without bread or soup. Was such a thing humanly possible? It was not possible. Not one of us even tried to resign himself to the prospect. But to whom could we turn?

This accursed affair of the ten lustres, coming on top of the affair of the three-quarters each, had shattered the last remnant of trust we had in the gentlefolk. On both occasions we had been deliberately cheated by the very man to whom we had entrusted our defence. There was no one whom we could trust. Where could we turn?

It is not easy to convey what that meant for us. A peasant would always consider himself as defenceless and helpless as a worm on the face of the earth if he could not gain entry to one or other of the cliques (whose leader would very likely be a lawyer) to which he knew he could turn to seek protection against the wiles of some other clique; or to find work, or get permission to emigrate, or ask a few days' leave for his soldier son, or ask advice about a will or a marriage settlement, and so forth.

Therefore every peasant had always tried to secure the influence of some member of the educated classes, a lawyer for choice; who would rely in turn on the good offices of a colleague who had some influence with the sub-prefect; who in turn would use his influence with the prefect; and so on, right up to the Government in Rome. The network of this vast conspiracy formed what educated people called the State. We hadn't seen it all so clearly before, but now our eyes were opened.

In the old days a peasant of Fontamara would not have dared apply at the public offices for, say, a birth certificate without being accompanied by Don Circostanza. If he went alone he would have been kicked out at once. General Baldissera remembered that in the early days of the railway from Rome to Pescara the inhabitants of Fontamara would solemnly present, not only the fare, but one of Don Circostanza's visiting cards each time they went to buy a railway ticket. After all, the railway belonged to the State, and had the State any obligations whatever towards the peasants? None at all. However, travelling got more common and the trains more and more crowded, so the custom of approaching the booking-clerk with a letter of recommendation gradually fell out of use. Peasants from Fontamara had actually travelled as far as Rome without mentioning it to Don Circostanza. But for everything else a peasant felt like a fish out of water without the protection of one of the gentle-folk.

It seemed to be the natural structure of society to us but in the memory of the oldest inhabitants things hadn't always been like this. Once upon a time there had been three or four large landowners, including the bishop, who owned and controlled everything on the basis of two or three simple laws, which everybody knew and understood. Then the Piedmontese came; and every day they made a new law and every day they appointed a new official, and in the end it all grew so complicated that you simply had to have a lawyer to be able to get along at all. Nominally the law was no longer for the landowners only, but was the same for everybody, but in practice, to enable you to take advantage of it, to dodge it, to use it for your own ends, the importance of the lawyers grew and grew.

When I was a boy there were two lawyers in our town, who also acted as notaries. Now there are four lawyers and eight notaries, to say nothing of all the muddlers who interfere in arbitration cases. All these lawyers are forced to invent feuds and dissensions in order to live; every week they provoke new lawsuits, and cause minor cases to drag out into long ones. Because of the lawyers, differences that in the old days were settled easily now dragged on for years, cost any amount of good money, and left long trails of rancour and hatred in their wake. Because of the lawyers, relations between one family and the next became more and more strained. The lawyers interfered in everything. Their gestures, their intonation, their style of dress, their manner of greeting, drinking and eating were specially studied to strike the imagination of the poor peasants.

The height of a peasant's ambition was to have a lawyer as godfather. Thus on confirmation days in the cathedral dozens of peasants' children, accompanied by their mothers in their Sunday best, would surround every lawyer of the town. Lawyers were the guests of honour at every family celebration, especially at wedding feasts, when they sat on the bride's right hand.

Each clique would stop at nothing in its perpetual warfare against every other. Each one would try to have the mayor, or the *podestà*, or the police magistrate or the captain of the gendarmes, or the sub-prefect, or the public prosecutor or the local deputy on its side. The prize that each clique longed for most was the disposal of the municipal and public charity funds. The clique in office would give jobs to its own protégés, impose taxes at random, filch the contracts for public works, and at election times the voters' lists would be loaded with names of absentees and dead men.

By such means it would frequently happen that one

clique would gain control of an entire village. Thus Fontamara had always been in the hands of Don Circostanza, Collarmele belonged to Don Cuccavascio, Ortona to Don Ciccone, Bisegna to Don Tarandella, and San Benedetto to Don Pomponio. Police magistrates, gendarmes, clerks might change; but the new ones would always have to submit to the clique or quit.

Quarrels between leaders of rival cliques turned into quarrels between whole villages. An example of this was the 'war' between Pescina and San Benedetto in 1913 – a war between rival leaders that the peasants fought with every possible weapon. They poisoned wells, cut down vines, set fire to sheaves of corn and ended up by shooting. The Government in Rome put an end to the 'war,' but with a great deal of difficulty. They sent a regiment of infantry and about a hundred horsemen. The war ended, but the hatred between the peasants remained.

The only peasants who remained outside the cliques were those who had nothing either to lose or to gain. These were either landless peasants or criminals who would not submit blindly to the orders of some master as domestic servants, rural guards, or, more recently, Fascists.

In recent years political parties had been formed in our part of the country, following the fashion set in other parts of the country. But the new political parties were nothing but the old cliques under new names. Thus, to reinforce his influence over the poorest peasants, Don Circostanza had had himself made leader of the People's Party, and represented himself as the champion of independence. He represented himself to us as the defender of the Marsica against the incursions of outside exploiters, but in the face of the real exploiter he had made a curious change of front.

Don Carlo Magna and the other big landowners had certainly suffered much at the hands of the bank. It was no longer they but the Contractor who fixed the prices at market. The Contractor systematically beat them in getting contracts for public works. The only matters in which they still had a say were those for which the Contractor cared nothing.

The big landowners tried to get back from the peasants what they lost because of the bank. At the same time they waged an underground war on the Contractor, instigating the peasants and the old public employees against him. The attitude of Don Circostanza and his colleagues towards the Contractor was entirely different. More cunning than the Contractor, knowing the minds of the peasants better than he, past-masters in the art of deceiving the poor, they had been trying to keep their influence by acting as intermediaries between the peasants and the new authorities. But in every moment of real difficulty Don Circostanza had come to the Contractor's rescue.

Certainly Don Circostanza had cheated us hundreds of times in the past. But he had always behaved towards us in a decent, friendly way. He always shook hands with us, and, when he was drunk, embraced us, and we had always forgiven him, all the more because we needed his protection. But the three-quarters each trick and the ten-lustres trick had definitely opened our eyes.

Everybody was against us. The old State, with its many rival conspiracies competing with each other, had come to an end. A new State, with one conspiracy only, had come in its place.

Where, then, were we to turn?

'We've reached a point when peasants have no bread and cobblers no boots and tailors have holes in their trousers, and bricklayers have no roof over their heads,' Baldissera went about preaching. 'We've reached the epoch of the bank. It's the end of everything. It's the reign of Antichrist.'

Not one of us was resigned to the loss of our water, but nobody knew the way to get it back. Ponzio Pilato and Michele Zompa wanted to start a lawsuit against the Contractor, but I wouldn't hear of it; nor would the others.

We knew only too well how that kind of lawsuit would end. It would last a century, go from one magistrate to another, from one appeal to another, eat up the resources of whole generations of peasants and in the end leave things exactly where they were before. Every village in the Marsica had known lawsuits like that between rich and poor. They ended only to begin all over again. But even if we did start a lawsuit, to whom could we entrust our case? To Don Circostanza? He would find another dodge, like that of the three-quarters each and the ten lustres. To Don Cuccavascio? To Don Tarandella? The less said about it the better.

All the same, no one was resigned to the loss of the water. No one was resigned to the loss of his entire crop. No one could reconcile himself to the prospect of winter without bread or soup.

'If there's no justice against thieves, we've reached the end of all things,' said Ponzio Pilato.

'When the law has broken down and the first to violate it are those whose business it is to enforce it, it's time to go back to the law of the people,' the old cobbler said one night.

'What is the law of the people?'

'God helps him who helps himself,' said Baldissera. Baldissera had ended by adopting the bitter doctrine of Berardo Viola.

Nobody contradicted him.

Raffaele Scarpone took a box of matches out of his pocket and said:

'This is the law of the people.'

Berardo said very little. Berardo was no longer his old self. His thoughts were elsewhere. His thoughts had been elsewhere ever since that first night with Elvira. Elvira was no longer in a fit state to get out of bed. She seemed to be slowly dying. In spite of that Berardo now spent every night with her, without even bothering to keep up appearances, almost under the eyes of her old, paralytic father.

'You'll kill the girl,' my wife said to him, but he only shrugged his shoulders.

The ten-lustres trick had left him quite indifferent. All our plans for vindicating our rights to the water left him cold.

'So much the worse for you,' he said. 'I've got no land to irrigate. I'm not a child any more, and I've got my own affairs to worry about.'

Berardo had one fixed idea: to go away, to emigrate, to work like a beast of the field, to work twice as hard as anybody else, and, after six months or a year, return to Fontamara and buy a piece of land and marry. You couldn't talk to him about anything else. He wasn't the same man any more.

All he wanted was to go away, to work ten hours a day, twelve hours a day, fourteen hours a day, and return with a thousand lire in his pocket.

Several times Berardo was seen talking to the Hero of Porta Pia about getting work in town.

'Heavy work, I mean; no getting jobs for servant girls and whores for me, and no work for Monsignor Calogero; and no Fascist work either. It's real work I want.'

The Hero wrote to various addresses in Rome and heard in reply that there were jobs going for navvies at ten lire a day.

'Ten lire a day isn't much,' Berardo came and told me, 'but it'll be the average pay. If I work more than the others, I shall be able to earn more. As for spending, I'll draw my belt tight – as tight as it'll go.'

Berardo asked me to lend him a hundred lire and I agreed, on condition that he took my son with him. Berardo accepted this. Elvira lent him another fifty lire.

On the eve of his departure I went to see Berardo to give him a few words of advice about my son. I found him, as usual, in the dyeing shop, sitting at the foot of the straw pallet on which Elvira lay.

'I don't want my son to do more than ten hours a day at heavy work,' I started saying to Berardo. 'I don't want him to stay at an inn where bad women go. . .'

At this point I was interrupted by Raffaele Scarpone dashing in. Some others who were with him waited outside.

'There's a revolution at Sulmona!' he shouted to Berardo as he entered.

'What sort of revolution?' Berardo asked. 'Have the confectioners rebelled?'

'No, the peasants have risen,' Scarpone answered, in the tone of a man in no mood to listen to jokes.

'Who told you that one?' Berardo asked.

'Baldissera.'

'Who told Baldissera?'

'That's a secret,' Scarpone replied.

'Then it's not true,' Berardo decided.

Scarpone went out into the street and told Venerdì Santo, who was one of those waiting outside, to go and fetch the cobbler. Nobody said a word while we waited.

Baldissera needed a lot of persuading, but he came in the end. This is what he told us:

'I went to the town today to buy leather. I met Donna Zizzola in the square. She was coming out of church. As you know, I worked in her parents' house when I was a boy. So we're on quite friendly terms, and we always stop and talk when we meet. "St. Anthony himself has sent you to me," Don Carlo Magna's wife said to me in a low voice. "Come to my house for a minute. I've got something I want to talk to you about."

'Knowing my duty, but without having the slightest idea what it was all about, I went to see her as soon as I had bought my leather. "Have you heard the great news?" she asked me as she opened the door. "There's a revolution at Sulmona. All the gendarmes have been sent there from here and from all around." There seems to have been a kind of

Contractor at Sulmona too, according to Donna Zizzola, who reduced everybody to ruin. The revolution began on the marketplace three days ago and is still going on. "Can it be that the day of reckoning has come for our brigand too?" Donna Zizzola asked, meaning, of course, our Contractor. But I didn't answer. "For two months I've burned two candles before the statue of St. Anthony night and day, praying that something might happen to him, but nothing has happened yet," she whispered in my ear. As I was still silent, she started talking more openly. "The time has come for action. The gendarmes are all at Sulmona. Hatred of the Contractor is widespread. We are only waiting for a sign. Only the peasants of Fontamara can give it. As I met you up there by the church I knew at once that you had been sent by St. Anthony himself." I explained to her that I had only come to town to buy leather, but Donna Zizzola's mind was on other things. "St. Anthony himself sent you," she insisted. "During my prayers this morning the saint directed me. He said: 'I can do nothing for you; only the peasants of Fontamara can give this robber the lesson he deserves'; and as I left the church I met you." '

Don Carlo Magna's wife told the old shoemaker that if the Fontamara peasants wanted petrol or arms they could have them, provided they applied through a trustworthy person.

As soon as Baldissera had finished Raffaele Scarpone turned to Berardo and said: 'Well, what about it?'

'What do you think about it yourself?' Berardo replied.

'Luigi Della Croce, Antonio Spaventa, Venerdì Santo, Gasparone, Antonio Zappa and I got together before we came here. They're just outside. In their name I tell you that we must follow the example of Sulmona. We mustn't refuse anyone's aid,' Raffaele said. He had already worked out a plan of campaign for a night attack on the town, to begin with the destruction of the many buildings belonging to the Contractor.

'But why do you want to do all this?' Berardo asked.

Raffaele lost his temper.

'Are you living in the moon, man?' he shouted. 'Have you forgotten all the wrongs that the Contractor has done us? Don't you know there's no other way left to us? Don't you know that this winter there'll be nothing to eat but stones?'

Berardo let him talk. Then he turned to Baldissera and said in the same calm, ingenuous tone as before:

'If Donna Zizzola hates the Contractor, why does she apply to St. Anthony for help? Hasn't she got a husband? And if St. Anthony shares Donna Zizzola's feelings, why does he turn to us? Hasn't he got an angel handy?'

Speaking in the same tone, he turned to Scarpone.

'If you burn the Contractor's factories down, do you suppose we can live on the ashes during the winter? If the workers in the Contractor's cement factory and the Contractor's brickworks and the Contractor's tannery lose their jobs, do you think we'll be any better off?'

Then he changed his tone and said what he really had on his mind. 'I tell you that all this doesn't concern me in the slightest. Our position is ugly enough in all conscience. Every man must look after his own affairs. In the past I've troubled myself about too many things which were no concern of mine. And now I'm thirty years old and own nothing but the straw I sleep on. I'm not a boy any longer and I've got my own affairs to think about. So leave me in peace!'

'It isn't we who stop you living in peace. It's the Contractor who stops us all from living in peace,' Scarpone replied.

'Hear, hear!' said Baldissera. 'No one wanted peace and quiet more than I did. But now there's neither law nor order, nor government nor justice. It's no time now for looking after your own affairs; nobody can be left in peace now. If the guardians of the law come by night and rape the women of your village, do you turn round and say: "Not one of those women is my wife?" If the guardians of the law take your

147

land and water away and prevent you from working, do you turn round and say: "That's no concern of mine?"'

Berardo stood listening, shaking his head. He knew all these arguments only too well. He had used them hundreds of times himself against General Baldissera. But he wasn't a boy any longer now. He hadn't only himself to think of now. He could no longer gaily set everything, including life and liberty, at stake, because he hadn't only himself to think of now. He was forced to think differently. Ever since that first night with Elvira he had been forced to think differently. The whole village had come round to Berardo's point of view just when he had forsaken it.

'Listen,' he said. 'Let me make myself perfectly clear, once and for all. I haven't got the slightest desire to go to gaol for your water and your land. I've got my own affairs to worry about.'

Scarpone and Baldissera got up and went away.

'Berardo's afraid,' said Scarpone to the young men waiting outside in the street, loudly enough for us all to hear.

Berardo was a demigod to the young men of Fontamara. They would willingly have followed him to death.

It was easy to see that nothing would happen without him.

All this time Elvira remained lying on her pallet, looking paler than ever. She hadn't taken her eyes off Berardo throughout the dispute. She had followed him, first with curiosity, as if she doubted whether he was in earnest, then with astonishment, and in the end, when doubt was no longer possible, with concern and alarm, though she did not dare interrupt or contradict him in the presence of the others. But after Scarpone and Baldissera had gone she could contain herself no longer and said to him in a tone full of reproach:

'If it's on my account that you're behaving like this, you might remember that what first attracted me to you a few years ago was that you argued just the other way round.'

When he saw that Elvira was against him too Berardo could not wholly restrain his anger and almost let out some frightful oath. But he turned on his heel and left without even saying good night.

It must have been midnight when I got home. 'Whatever happens, you try and go to sleep. You're leaving tomorrow before daylight,' I said to my son.

We all tried to go to sleep, or pretended we were going to sleep. But not one of us managed to. All three of us were lying awake when, about two o'clock, we suddenly heard the church bell ringing. The first and second chimes were clear and strong. Those that followed sounded like echoes of the first.

'Did you hear?' My wife started up in alarm.

'It must be Our Lady,' I told her. 'Let's go to sleep.'

It wasn't an honest answer. We all three went on listening, holding our breath. But we heard no more.

Perhaps another half-hour passed, and then we heard two or three more chimes of the bell, weaker than the first.

' Did you hear?' my wife said, more terrified than ever.

'It must be the wind,' I said. 'Let's go to sleep.'

But the air was calm, and it couldn't have been the wind. Besides, not even the strongest north wind had ever rung our church bell.

A little later we heard another chime, this time so faint that we only heard it because we were listening.

'It must be an owl,' I said, just for the sake of saying something.

'How can an owl ring a church bell?'

'If it isn't an owl it must be a weasel.'

'What can a weasel be doing in the church tower?'

'If it isn't a weasel it must be a witch,' was the only thing that I could think of.

At that moment there could have been few people asleep in Fontamara. And all those who were lying awake because of the unaccountable ringing of the church bell were probably making the same conjectures and having the same arguments about it as we were. But everyone minded his own business and no one got up to see who was in the church tower.

My son will tell you what happened next.

9 At four o'clock next morning Berardo and I left Fontamara and set off to the local town to catch the train to Rome.

Berardo was in a bad mood. He didn't even answer my 'Good morning'. I behaved as if I hadn't noticed it, as I didn't want any unpleasantness right at the beginning of the journey.

'Did you hear the bell last night?' I asked him, trying to start a conversation. I might have been talking to the wind. Just before we reached the chapel of Our Lady of the Floods I tried again.

'Do you think it's raining in Rome?' I said, but he didn't answer.

He hurried along with enormous strides, and I had my work cut out to keep up with him. As we entered the town we suddenly heard the whistle of a train. We ran to catch it, but it was a goods train and there was a long time to wait until ours arrived.

We had been sitting in the waiting-room for half an hour when Raffaele Scarpone appeared at the door.

Berardo pretended not to see him. He turned his back on him and started reading a notice stuck on the wall. But Scarpone went straight up to him.

'Teofilo has hanged himself,' he said.

Berardo did not move his eyes from the notice.

'General Baldissera found him on the stairs of the church tower with the bell-rope round his neck,' Scarpone went on. 'His body was still warm. He must have been swinging on the rope all night.'

'May he rest in peace,' Berardo said, without turning his head.

'I've been to Don Abbacchio's,' Scarpone went on, as if he did not believe Berardo's indifference. 'I've just come from Don Abbacchio's house. At first he just cursed me for waking him so early, then he refused to come and give the Absolution. "How can you refuse the blessing to a sacristan who has served the Church all his life?" I asked him. "A man who hangs himself goes straight to hell," Don Abbacchio said. "If he's a sacristan he goes to the bottommost pit." '

Berardo was unmoved.

'May he rest in peace,' he said once more.

'We're going to put Teofilo right in the middle of the church,' Scarpone went on. 'If the priest doesn't come we'll have to do without him. If he sends the gendarmes we'll keep them off. We're going to put Teofilo in the middle of the church and leave him there for twenty-four hours, so that Christ, Our Lady, San Rocco, St. Anthony, Joseph, San Berardo and all the other saints will have time to see him. They will see what straits we've come to. . .'

'May he rest in peace,' Berardo repeated.

Our train came in.

'Don't go,' Scarpone said suddenly.

'Why not?' asked Berardo, surprised.

'Don't go,' repeated Scarpone.

Berardo went towards the train. I followed him. Scarpone followed me, shaking his head, bewildered.

'The gendarmes will be coming for Teofilo,' Scarpone said. 'Don't go, Berardo.'

But we went.

We didn't exchange a word during the whole journey. Berardo sat opposite me the whole time, gazing out of the window. I watched him. I suddenly realised that he would stop at nothing to gain his ends. No scruple would hold him back. He would have had no hesitation in throwing me out of the window if that had served his purpose. The set of his jaw was enough to frighten you. 'If he's hungry, he'll eat me alive,' I thought to myself.

We put up in Rome at the Inn of the Penitent Thief. This inn had a sign showing the three crosses of Calvary. You might have imagined that the inn took its name from the famous thief who was crucified on Christ's right hand and recognised Him before he died and was rewarded with the great promise: 'Today shalt thou be with Me in Paradise.' But in reality the inn was named after its proprietor. Its proprietor, after several imprisonments for theft, just like the Hero of Porta Pia, had, towards the end of his life, thrown in his lot with the Fascists and taken part in a large number of punitive expeditions against enemies of the new regime, specialising in patriotic robberies from co-operative stores and trades unions. So meritorious were his services that the Chief of Police himself granted him the title of 'The Penitent Thief' at a patriotic ceremony.

Early next day we went to an office in the Via Venti Settembre, from which we hoped to get work as navvies.

The porter sent us up to the third floor. We went there and found a passage full of waiting people. We joined the queue. Our turn came towards midday, and we then found we had been lining up on the fourth floor and not on the third.

Next day we went back to the third floor. We waited there for three hours, sitting on a bench, the two of us alone. Many people walked past us, but no one took any notice of us. Finally we were sent up to the fifth floor. We waited there for two hours and were then given an address in the Corso Vittorio. So ended the third day.

In the office in the Corso Vittorio they asked us: 'Have you got your papers?'

'What papers?' we answered in surprise.

We were taken to a window where a clerk made out our papers for us and stuck twelve stamps on them, one for each month of the year.

The clerk asked us for thirty-five lire.

'Pay, always pay,' Berardo grumbled. Thirty-five cuts with a knife would not have hurt us more. We paid up.

Then we went back to the office where we had been before.

'Here are our papers,' we said.

'All right,' we were told. 'Go to the employment exchange tomorrow and sign on as unemployed and as volunteers for work on public reclamation schemes.'

So ended the fourth day.

I must admit that Berardo put up with all this very patiently. He seemed to take it all for granted.

'The harder it is to get work the more we'll earn when we get it,' he said to me over and over again.

In the afternoons, when the offices were closed, he took me for walks all over the city.

'Look, look!' he shouted excitedly the first time we came across a building with the word 'bank' written up outside it.

Berardo stared at it, fascinated, for some minutes. Then he whispered in my ear:

'That's where the Contractor gets all his money from.'

But farther on we came across another bank, and then a third and then a fourth. After a bit we stopped counting them. Which one of them belonged to the Contractor? It was hard to say. In the middle of Rome, where we expected to find St. Peter's, we found nothing but banks.

'Just look, just look!' Berardo exclaimed each time we

came across a new bank. Each was bigger and more impressive than the last. Around each there was a great coming and going of men and motor-cars.

Berardo never tired of wondering at it all.

One evening we found a great crowd outside our inn. A military forage cart had overturned and was lying on its side up against a wall. A number of people were trying to move it. They were making a lot of noise, but not doing any good, as is the usual way with town crowds.

Berardo pushed his way through the mob, took off his hat and coat, went down on his knees, crept under the cart and took the weight on his back. To everyone's astonishment and admiration, he slowly lifted the cart and put it on its wheels again

This incident seemed to restore a little of Berardo's old talkativeness. 'Donna Zizzola burns two candles before the statue of St. Anthony to destroy the power of the banks. Isn't it ridiculous?' he said to me that evening.

I was in no mood for an argument. I realised that Berardo wanted to reopen the discussion he'd had with Scarpone on the eve of his departure. I wasn't in a mood to discuss anything.

'Hare-brained escapades are all right as long as you're young,' he went on. 'There's some sense in roasting chestnuts, but what's the good of burning the Contractor's house down?'

I let him talk, as he seemed to want to.

'Don't you see that bravery has got nothing whatever to do with it?' he went on. 'Scarpone may think I'm afraid, but he's wrong. Do you think I wouldn't risk my life to earn a little more than the others? I feel I've got strength to do things nobody has ever done before. They'll give us work tomorrow, and when we start you'll be surprised, and so will the others, and the foreman will be surprised too.'

'I wonder how Teofilo's burial went off?' I said, to stop his ravings. The interruption annoyed him.

'I tell you bravery has got nothing whatever to do with it!' he shouted angrily. 'Nor has violence got anything to do with it. Did the Contractor use violence against us? He did not. He didn't use courage or violence, he used his wits. That's how he got the stream from us. He didn't even take it. Fontamara actually gave it to him. First they got the signatures to the petition to the Government, then he pulled off the three-quarters-each trick, and then the ten-lustres trick. What else could you have expected the Contractor to do? He acted perfectly legally and put his own interests first.'

Such was the extent to which Berardo had shifted his point of view.

'The price of land is certain to go down a lot,' he went on, revealing his innermost thoughts. 'Without the stream the price of land is bound to fall. It will have to be cultivated differently too.'

He already knew the bit of land he wanted when he went home again.

On the morning of the fifth day we went to the employment exchange to get work.

'What province do you come from?' we were asked.

'Aquila,' we said.

'Then you must apply to the Aquila exchange.'

'Where is the Aquila exchange?'

The clerk burst out laughing. He repeated our question to the other clerks and the whole office roared with laughter.

'The Aquila employment exchange is in Aquila,' the clerk told us, after he had quietened down again and wiped his eyes after laughing so much.

But we hadn't the slightest desire to tour Italy.

'We've been to enough offices by this time,' Berardo declared emphatically. 'We came to Rome to get work and not for a Calvary.' But our Calvary went on.

A lawyer from the Abruzzi, named the Hon. Don Achille Pazienza, lived at the Inn of the Penitent Thief. We promptly applied to him. On the sixth day of our stay at Rome he summoned us to an interview in his bedroom, which was next to ours, and as dark, narrow, untidy and dirty as ours. Don Achille Pazienza was lying on his bed; he was a poor, wheezy old man, with a ten-day beard, a yellow suit, white linen shoes, a straw hat on his head, a bronze medal on his chest and a wooden tooth-pick in his mouth. He had dressed up like that to receive us. Under the bed stood a chamber-pot full to the brim.

'A consultation costs ten lire,' Don Pazienza started by saying.

'Oh, all right,' I answered desperately.

'The ten lire is payable in advance,' Don Pazienza said.

We handed over ten lire.

'Ten lire each,' he added.

We gave him another ten lire.

Whereupon the old gentleman rose from his bed and left the room without saying a word. We heard him coughing in the passage. Then we heard the cough slowly go down the stairs, stop for a few minutes at the bottom, where the Penitent Thief was on the watch, go out into the street and fade away as the old man entered the inn on the opposite side of the road.

We had to wait for nearly an hour before the cough turned up again. Once more we heard it cross the street, slowly and wearily creep up the stairs and hesitate for a moment outside our door. Then the old man came in with a loaf of bread, half a sausage and half a bottle of red wine. 'Yours is a bad case,' the Hon. Pazienza said to us after taking up his position again on the bed. We hadn't yet told him what we had come to him about.

'How much money have you got left?' he asked us after a long, thoughtful pause.

We put everything we had left, including the coppers, into Berardo's hat. It added up to about fourteen lire.

'Your case is not only insignificant, but hopeless,' said the lawyer, disappointed. 'Can you get more money from

157

Fontamara?' he asked, after another thoughtful pause.

'Of course,' Berardo answered, though he was sure of the contrary.

'And perhaps a chicken? Just a chicken or two? And some cheese? And a little honey for my cough?' the old man added.

'Of course,' Berardo answered hurriedly, though he had never seen honey in his life.

'You've got a perfectly clear case,' the lawyer said with a smile, in the course of which he showed us at least forty yellowish teeth.

Berardo then explained our position.

Don Pazienza arose, looked for his stick, which looked for all the world like an old umbrella handle, brandished it in the air, and said: 'Come with me.'

We went with him. The first stop was at the post office.

Don Pazienza wrote out a telegram as follows:

'Send 200 lire, 7 lbs. cheese, 2 lbs. honey, some chickens.'

'How shall I address it? Which of you has the richer family?' he asked.

'Address it to my father, Vincenzo Viola,' said Berardo, who had lost his father when he was a child.

Don Pazienza was just about to send the telegram when Berardo tapped him on the shoulder.

'Don't you like peaches, sir?' he said.

'Very much indeed,' has the answer. 'They're excellent for coughs.'

So a request for 7 lbs. of peaches was added to the telegram. The lawyer copied it out. 'Pay for the telegram and come with me,' he said to us.

We paid for the telegram and went with him. The next stop was at the Fascist employment exchange, from which we had been sent away on the first day. Don Pazienza left us standing in the passage. We saw him through a window talking to an official and gesticulating excitedly. He showed the official the telegram which had been sent to Fontamara and pointed out the most important words with his finger. The official seemed to have some strong objections to offer, because our lawyer suddenly went pale. He rushed back to us and asked:

'Is Fontamara cheese for cooking or for eating?'

'When it's fresh it's for eating and when it's stale it's for cooking,' Berardo answered, to the great satisfaction of the lawyer, who repeated our reassuring reply to the official.

Apparently there were no more hitches, because Don Pazienza came back and said to us:

'Things are moving. The employment exchange will require the necessary documents: birth certificates, police records and good conduct certificates. As soon as you've got them your names will be placed on the Unemployed Register. The work will follow. The employment exchange will send for you themselves.'

On the seventh day of our stay in Rome we only had four lire left.

We bought two loaves of bread and then we hadn't a cent left.

'News from the employment exchange can't be long now,' Berardo kept on telling me, to keep up his own courage.

We no longer moved from the inn, so as to be ready when the summons from the employment exchange came. Besides, we were now far too hungry to want to go for any more walks.

At every sound of footsteps we rushed to the door.

As soon as we saw the postman we dashed downstairs to the ground floor, where the Penitent Thief was on the watch.

The Hon. Pazienza shared our anxiety. The only difference was that we were waiting for work, while he was waiting for a money order and provisions from Berardo's father. All three of us stayed in bed all day and all three of us dashed downstairs at every sound. On the way up again mutual recriminations grew more bitter every day.

'You've got a heartless father,' Don Pazienza would say to Berardo. 'How can he take such a long time over sending you a mere two hundred lire?'

'Is there any work or not?' Berardo would answer. 'If there is any work, why don't they send for us? If there is any work why are there so many formalities?'

'I can understand the delay so far as the provisions are concerned,' the lawyer would say. 'Parcels always travel slowly, especially if the contents are perishable. But a money order ought to arrive the same day. Your father is a selfish pig.'

'What has a birth certificate to do with getting a job?' Berardo would reply. 'If a man is looking for work it's obvious that he must have been born. Nobody has ever wanted work before he was born!'

After three days' fasting and waiting Berardo and I gave up dashing downstairs whenever we heard the postman.

We lay in bed from morning till night and only got up to go and drink water from the tap in the lavatory. Don Pazienza was much more patient and hopeful than we. Three times a day, at every post, we heard his cough move from his bed, leave his room, go slowly downstairs until it reached the ground floor and, after a time, slowly and wearily come up again, and pause by our door, outside the keyhole. Then we would hear the old man muttering curses at Fontamara.

'Berardo Viola,' panted the poor old man, 'your father is a pig. Your father is my ruin, Berardo Viola. Your father will be the death of me. I've eaten nothing for three days because of your father. It's all his fault.'

Berardo did not answer. He had relapsed into his former silence. He would stare up at the ceiling for hours on end without saying a word.

'What shall we do?' I asked. 'We can't go on for ever without anything to eat.'

But Berardo didn't answer.

On the fourth day of our fast we had an unexpected thrill. It must have been about five o'clock. We heard both Don Pazienza and the Penitent Thief coming up the stairs, shouting wildly.

We heard the lawyer singing:

Oh, where are Victory's golden wings?
God made her slave of Rome. . .

They came to our door, pushed it open without knocking and walked in. The Penitent Thief was flourishing a telegram for Berardo, and Don Pazienza was carrying two bottles of wine.

'Berardo Viola,' the lawyer cried, 'your father is a fine fellow. The money order has arrived!'

'Really?' said Berardo in astonishment, almost beside himself with joy. Of course, he didn't believe it was his father, who had been dead for twenty years, who had sent him a money order. But after four days' fasting you're ready to believe almost anything.

While the lawyer opened the bottles of wine Berardo took the telegram, opened it, read it, looked at us, folded it up and put it in his pocket without saying a word.

'What is it?' I asked.

Berardo didn't answer. His face was like a mask. The whites of his eyes had suddenly become thick and bloodshot. I knew, from Fontamara, that this was the only outward sign he gave of strong emotion.

'What is it?' I asked again, in the friendliest way I could.

Berardo stretched himself out on the bed without saying a word. The Penitent Thief and Don Pazienza went away, taken completely aback, but not forgetting the two bottles of wine. I lay down next to Berardo, on the same bed, and remained still for a long time, to gain his confidence. Then I asked him again:

'What is it? What has happened? Has anybody died?'

161

But he did not answer. I realised that somebody must have died at Fontamara.

At eight o'clock the same evening there was a sudden commotion in the room next to ours, which was occupied, as I have told you, by Don Pazienza. Immediately afterwards our door was opened and Don Pazienza appeared. He didn't come in, but shouted at us:

'The head of the Fascist employment exchange has just been to see me. Your papers have come. Your certificate, signed by the *podestà*, stated: "Conduct, worst possible from the national point of view." You can't be given work with a certificate like that! You'll never get work with a certificate like that! Besides, the police have been notified.'

He slammed the door and went away.

Five minutes later the door was opened again. It was the Penitent Thief. 'Your room has been let,' he told us. 'You've got half an hour to clear out.'

It was dark when we left the inn.

'What shall we do now?' I asked Berardo. But what could he answer me? Nothing.

My legs felt very weak and my head ached from hunger. Every now and then I thought I was going to faint. People in the street stared at us. They moved aside, as if they were frightened of us. Berardo's appearance was really terrifying.

We found ourselves, without meaning to, near the station. There were a large number of gendarmes, soldiers and police, stopping and questioning passers-by in the square. They held up motor-cars and searched them too. Suddenly a young man, after looking at us in astonishment, stopped in front of us.

'Good evening,' he said to Berardo.

Berardo looked at him suspiciously and did not answer.

'I was just thinking about you,' the young man went on. 'If I hadn't met you here I was going to see you at Fontamara tomorrow.'

'I haven't got a penny in the world,' Berardo said. 'If you

want to cheat anyone you had better find somebody else.'

The young man began to laugh. He looked half student, half workman. He was tall and thin and was well but not smartly dressed. His voice and appearance did not invite suspicion.

'Don't you remember the last time you were at Avezzano?' he asked Berardo. 'Don't you remember the inn where you and the other men from Fontamara were taken by the red-haired police spy with the scar on his chin? Don't you remember? Have you forgotten who put you on your guard against him?'

Berardo looked at him hard and then recognised him.

'Give us some money to buy food,' I asked him, when I saw that Berardo was going to let the opportunity slip.

The young man from Avezzano led us to a coffeeshop and ordered ham and eggs.

'Is that for us?' Berardo asked suspiciously. 'Who's going to pay? We haven't got any money.'

To reassure him the young man went to the desk and paid the bill in advance. In the meantime Berardo looked at me, as if to say: 'This fellow must be a lunatic.'

'What are all the gendarmes and militia up to?' Berardo asked the young man after he'd had something to eat.

'It's the usual hunt for the Mystery Man,' the young man said, but this didn't mean anything to us.

'For some time an unknown person, called the Mystery Man, has been endangering public safety,' the young man explained. 'The Mystery Man is mentioned in every case before the Special Tribunal. He prints pamphlets and distributes them secretly. Everyone caught carrying illegal papers and documents always admits having received them from the Mystery Man. First the Mystery Man used to work at a few big factories, then in the city suburbs and the barracks. Then he put in an appearance at the university. One morning he was reported to have been at several places at once, and on the same day he was reported to be on the frontier. The best detectives in Italy have been put on his track, but they haven't found him yet. They've made six thousand arrests, and time after time the Government have believed that the Mystery Man was among the prisoners. But after a brief interval the secret press gets to work again and the Mystery Man again appears in the records of the Special Tribunal. He seems to have been in the Abruzzi for some time past.'

'In the Abruzzi?' Berardo asked eagerly.

'In Sulmona, Prezza, Avezzano and in other places too. Wherever he appears the peasants revolt; wherever the peasants revolt he turns up.'

'But who is he? Is he the Devil?' Berardo asked.

'He may be,' the man from Avezzano answered, laughing.

'If only someone would show him the way to Fontamara,' Berardo added.

'He already knows it,' the man from Avezzano answered quietly.

At that moment a policeman and a squad of militia entered the coffee-shop and came up to us.

'Papers and identity cards,' they demanded.

The militia searched the coffeeshop while the policeman went through the papers we had got from the employment exchange and examined the personal papers, identity card and many other papers as well belonging to the young man who was with us.

Our papers were in order, and the policeman was just leaving when the militia rushed up to us with a parcel wrapped up in a piece of cloth which was lying at the foot of the hat stand. Its contents turned the policeman and the militia into raging furies. They rushed at us, shouting: 'Whom does this packet belong to? Who dropped it?'

They arrested us and took us to the police station without waiting for any explanations.

Berardo thought the parcel contained stolen property and that they took us for thieves. The whole way to the police station he shouted:

'We're not thieves! You ought to be ashamed of your-selves! You're thieves! We're the people who've been robbed, not the thieves! The Fascist employment exchange are the thieves; they stole thirty-five lire from us. Don Pazienza is a thief – he took twenty lire from us. We're not thieves. The Contractor is a thief!'

At the police station a continuous stream of prisoners was being brought in from all over the city.

'The hunt for the Mystery Man is still going on,' the young man from Avezzano explained to Berardo in a whis-per. When Berardo grasped the fact that we had not been arrested as thieves he quietened down.

After a few formalities we were locked in a cell in which there were two other prisoners already. Berardo and I exchanged a glance of satisfaction. At least we had a roof over our heads and were sure of something to eat tomorrow. There was time to think about the more distant future.

Half of the cell was taken up with a block of concrete, which was just a little higher than the floor and served as a bed. In a corner there was a hole, the object of which was even more obvious.

The two prisoners who were in the cell before us lay stretched out in the other corner, using their rolled-up coats for pillows. I followed their example at once. I lay down on the concrete, took off my coat and put it under my head. Berardo and the man from Avezzano started talking eagerly, striding up and down the cell. The man from Avezzano spoke in a whisper, no doubt because of the other two men, but Berardo was too excited to follow his example. So I could only follow what Berardo said.

'This Mystery Man yarn doesn't convince me. Is this Mystery Man a townsman or a peasant? If he's a townsman and goes to the Abruzzi he must have an ulterior motive. . .

'But townspeople are well off,' he went on. 'They're well off because they exploit the peasants. Oh, yes, I know there are poor people in towns too. Peppino Goriano had a bad time, and the lawyer Pazienza isn't exactly wallowing in luxury either. But they're not real townspeople; they're people from the Abruzzi who've come to town!'

At times Berardo tried to whisper, and I lost the thread of the conversation, but I could see from their gestures that he and the man from Avezzano were not agreeing. Berardo, although no doubt it would have been better to drop his voice, sometimes burst out in his excitement, and then not only could our two fellow-prisoners hear him, but most probably those in the neighbouring cells could hear him too.

'You say there were newspapers in the parcel they found in the coffee-shop? Do you mean printed papers? What can a paper parcel like that be worth?'

The young man was not only a decent fellow but a patient one too. He advised Berardo to lower his voice, and Berardo promised, but very soon he couldn't help starting to shout again.

'But townspeople are well off and the peasants are not. The townspeople eat well and drink well and don't pay taxes. Townspeople do hardly any work and earn a lot of money. Twenty lire a day for beating people up and not being beaten themselves. You've only got to look at what they make us pay for hats, clothes and shoe-leather . . . We peasants are like worms. Everyone preys on us. Everyone tramples on us. Everyone cheats us. Even Don Circostanza turned against us. Even Don Circostanza!'

The man from Avezzano listened intently to all this.

'It's terrible,' he muttered. 'Is all that you say true? Do all the peasants think the same way as you?'

'I don't understand,' Berardo went on again soon afterwards. 'I don't understand why townspeople should have printed a paper and given it away to the peasants for nothing. I don't understand either why the Mystery Man doesn't look after his own affairs. Or perhaps he's a paper merchant and prints newspapers to use up his paper?

'And all these people you're telling me about who go to

166

prison – are they mad?' I heard Berardo asking. 'And if they're not mad, what are they driving at? And those you've mentioned who were shot by the Government – what were they getting at? Is getting shot their way of looking after their own affairs?'

The young man from Avezzano must have realised that the many objections he was putting up were objections he was putting up to himself. All the hopes Berardo had had of looking after his own affairs, of finding work and then buying a bit of land, had vanished. All the ways were blocked. The *podestà* had described us as very bad from the national point of view, and so all ways were blocked. So Berardo must have felt his old way of thinking taking possession of him again, this time more strongly than ever. The objections which he was putting up to the man from Avezzano were his last stand.

The talk must have gradually shifted to other countries, including Russia, and I heard Berardo say:

'Russia? Tell me the truth. Is there really such a place as this Russia which they talk such a lot about? Everybody talks about Russia, but no one has ever been there. Peasants go everywhere – to America, Africa, France. But no one has ever been to Russia.'

On some points Berardo was unshakable – for instance, when the talk turned to the question of freedom.

'Freedom of speech?' Berardo asked. 'We're not lawyers. Freedom of the Press? We're not printers. Why don't you talk of freedom to work, freedom to own land?'

At that point I must have fallen asleep without noticing it. I must have been asleep for some hours when Berardo woke me. He was sitting at my feet, with the young man beside him.

I was surprised they were still awake and still talking.

'I'm sorry,' Berardo said to me. 'I'll let you go to sleep again in a few minutes. Do you know the true story of Prince Torlonia?'

'I'm not interested,' I told him. 'All true stories about

princes are the same to me. Let me go to sleep.'

'I must tell you that the so-called Prince Torlonia is not a prince and his name isn't Torlonia either.'

'You must be dreaming,' I answered.

'I must tell you that the so-called Prince Torlonia whom the peasants worship as the lord of the earth came to Italy a hundred years ago as a camp-follower of a French regiment. Not only was he not a prince, but he hadn't a handle to his name, like Don Pazienza, even. He was a wine and sausage dealer. His name wasn't Torlonia, but Torlogne. He was a Frenchman, a speculator. He speculated in war, he speculated in salt; he made money out of the priests and out of the Piedmontese. He robbed right and left and was made a duke and then a prince. . .'

'Are you dreaming?' I asked Berardo.

But Berardo turned his back on me and started talking to the man from Avezzano. They no longer disagreed. From his speech and gestures it was obvious that Berardo had given up making objections. He was his old self again.

What he had told me about Torlonia was like a fairy-tale to me, but the old Berardo was fond of such fairy-tales.

I fell asleep again while they went on talking. When I woke again it was daylight. Berardo was striding up and down the cell like a caged lion. The man from Avezzano was lying at my side, but wasn't asleep. He was lying close to me, as if he had been waiting for me to wake up.

'Do you trust Berardo?' he whispered to me.

'Yes,' I told him.

'Every peasant ought to trust him,' the young man went on. 'You must tell everybody in Fontamara to trust him. He is an extraordinary man. It is fortunate that he has gone through what he has gone through. I don't believe there is another peasant like him in the whole of Italy. You must tell them that at Fontamara. Do what Berardo tells you. You two will be set free today or tomorrow and sent home, no doubt. My fate may be different. Excuse me if I don't explain now.

Berardo will explain at Fontamara. The first thing to do is to reconcile Berardo with Raffaele Scarpone. Berardo knows the rest.'

At eight o'clock they brought us a can of coffee. Berardo interrupted his march up and down the cell.

'I want to speak to the commissary of police at once,' he said to the warder.

'Wait your turn,' he answered and went away.

These words did not escape the young man from Avezzano and he looked at Berardo with eyes full of terror. He did not dare ask him for an explanation, but fear of betrayal was in his eyes.

At nine o'clock the three of us were taken before the commissary of police.

Berardo stepped forward and said:

'I am ready to tell everything, sir.'

'Carry on,' said the commissary of police.

'The parcel of forbidden papers found in the coffeeshop near the station belonged to me. I had the sheets printed to distribute them among the peasants. I am the Mystery Man!'

10   So the Mystery Man had been captured at last.

At the news that the Mystery Man had been captured, journalists, Fascist chiefs and high State officials flocked to the police station where we were imprisoned. So the Mystery Man was a peasant.

The police had been searching for him in the city, but was there a single one of its inhabitants who was unknown to them? Every single one of them was filed, rubber-stamped, card-indexed, watched and known. Those known to be hostile to the Government were particularly thoroughly filed, rubber-stamped, card-indexed, watched and known. But the peasants? Who knew the peasants? Has there ever been a Government in Italy which has known the peasants? And how could they have card-indexed, rubber-stamped, watched and known every single peasant?

So the Mystery Man was a peasant. Every now and then Berardo was fetched from the cell to be shown to yet another high official who wanted to question him, or merely to see him. As a precaution Berardo, the man from Avezzano and I were separated during the night and put in three different cells, but during the next few days they brought us up all together several times for special interrogations.

The commissary of police wanted to know a great deal from Berardo. He wanted to know where the secret printing works were, who the printer was and whether he had accomplices. But Berardo would not answer. Berardo bit his lips till they bled to show that he wasn't going to speak.

At every interrogation he looked worse. At the first interrogation he had just one blue mark under his right eye, but later on he was hardly recognisable. Lips, nose, ears and eyebrows bore the marks of violence. But still he would not speak. He would not answer the police commissary's questions. When he could no longer close his torn lips he clenched his teeth to show the police commissary his determination not to speak.

One day I was sent for, for a special interrogation too. I was taken to a cellar and thrown down on a wooden bench and my hands were bound behind my back with a leather belt. Then it was as if a rain of fire were falling on my back, as if a hole had been made in my back and fire were being poured in, as if a bottomless pit were being torn open inside me.

When I came round I saw that blood had been oozing out of my mouth and forming a little rivulet on the bench. I licked it with the tip of my tongue, because my throat was burning.

The next day the man from Avezzano was released.

Berardo and I were put back into the same cell, together with a man who had every appearance of being a police spy. I whispered my suspicion into Berardo's ear, but he answered:

'It doesn't matter a bit. I've already said everything I should have said.'

But when I told him that the man from Avezzano had been released, he said:

'Now we'd better find a way of getting out, too. This

game's all right if it doesn't last too long.'

It had been easy enough to start the game, but it wasn't going to be so easy to end it.

When Berardo told the police commissary that his first confession had been false, the commissary sent him back to his cell, with a laugh, saying:

'Either confess everything you know, or things'll go badly with you.'

The same evening Berardo was sent for, for yet another special interrogation. Berardo's special interrogations had a special quality of horror. Berardo would resist. He was incapable of taking a blow without returning it. Eight or nine warders were needed to bind his hands and feet. That evening he pretended to be resigned to the torture without making any resistance. But while a warder was bending over him, tying a rope round his knees, he fell on him and bit the nape of his neck, gripping so firmly with his teeth that the other warders had to hammer his jaws to make him let go. Finally they brought him back to his cell, carrying him by the feet and shoulders, like Christ after He was taken down from the Cross.

'He's outside and I'm in here,' Berardo said to me next morning. 'After all, he's a townsman at heart, too. He's outside, enjoying himself, now, and I'm in here. I'm getting myself killed here for his sake. Why don't I tell everything – everything I know, and everything that I don't know and only imagine, and on top of that everything I don't know and don't even imagine?'

(The prisoner whom we suspected of being a spy pricked up his ears.)

The next time we were called before the commissary of police I thought Berardo, for the sake of getting out of prison, was going to tell everything the man from Avezzano had told him. I couldn't make up my mind whether this was wise on his part or not.

'Are you ready to confess everything?' the commissary of

police asked him.

'Yes,' Berardo answered.

The commissary of police held before him a newspaper that had the following headline in big letters:

LONG LIVE BERARDO VIOLA!

'This secretly printed newspaper contains a good deal of information on the treatment you have rightly undergone at the hands of the police, from the day of your arrest until today,' said the police commissary. 'Since you are now ready to confess, begin by telling us how you have managed to transmit news to this clandestine newspaper from your cell.'

Berardo made no reply.

'There's a great deal about Fontamara in this newspaper,' the commissary went on. 'The diversion of a stream from its course is mentioned, a grazing ground is mentioned, the Fucino question is mentioned, the suicide of a certain Teofilo is mentioned, and the death of a certain Elvira, and so on. It's obvious that no one but an inhabitant of Fontamara could have written it. Explain how you managed to transmit all this to the clandestine newspaper from your cell.'

Berardo made no reply. He gazed as if hypnotised at the newspaper that the police commissary held before his eyes, the newspaper that contained his name and Elvira's name and, in bold headlines: 'Long live Berardo Viola!'

'Speak up, man,' the commissary insisted.

'I cannot,' said Berardo. 'I would rather die.'

The commissary continued to exhort him to speak. But Berardo was already elsewhere in spirit. He no longer saw the commissary of police, he no longer heard him. He was led back to his cell like someone who has made his will and is ready to die.

That night neither of us slept.

Berardo held his head in his hands as if it were about to burst. He made up his mind to confess. Then he changed his mind. Then he made up his mind again. Then he changed it.

He held his head in his hands, as if to prevent its bursting. Why should he stay in prison? Why should he die in prison at thirty years of age? For honour? For an ideal? But when had he ever taken an interest in politics? Whole hours passed like this. So spoke Berardo Viola, to himself and to me, while the third occupant of the cell strained to catch every word. The struggle within him went on.

'If I turn traitor, everything is lost,' he said. 'If I turn traitor, Fontamara will be damned for ever. If I turn traitor, centuries will pass before such an opportunity occurs again. And if I die? . . . I shall be the first peasant to die not for himself, but for others. For the other peasants. For the unity of the peasants.'

That was his great discovery. That word seemed to lift the scales from his eyes, as if a brilliant light had suddenly been brought inside our cell.

'Unity,' he said. 'What is unity? Have you ever heard the word? It's a new word. Unity. That is, solidarity. That is, strength. That is, liberty. That is, land (rent-free!). Have you ever heard that word? Such a simple thing. You must take that word back to Fontamara. If I die' – he said to me – 'you must take that word back to Fontamara. Unity. You must tell them all – Raffaele Scarpone first of all, and then all the others, Michele Zompa, General Baldissera, Ponzio Pilato, Antonio Ranocchia, and all the rest. Unity. An end must be put to hatred between peasant and peasant. Away with hatred between peasants and workers. There's only one thing that we lack – unity. All the rest will come by itself.'

Those were the last words I heard Berardo speak. Next morning we were separated for the last time.

Two days later I was summoned by the police commissary, who was unusually gentle.

'Berardo Viola committed suicide last night,' he told me. 'He hanged himself in despair from the window of his cell. There's no question about the facts, but there is no evidence. A witness is absolutely indispensable. Are you willing to sign a statement to the effect that Berardo hanged himself last night? If you are, you will be set at liberty at once.'

On hearing that Berardo was dead, I burst into tears.

The commissary prepared the statement, and I signed it, without reading it. Then I was taken to the office of the chief of police.

'Were you the friend of Berardo Viola, the deceased?' he asked me.

'Yes, sir.'

'Do you agree that the deceased always had suicidal tendencies?'

'Yes, sir.'

'Do you agree that recently the deceased had a serious disappointment in love?'

'Yes, sir.'

'Do you agree that the deceased was confined in the same cell as you and hanged himself from a window-bar while you were asleep?'

'Yes, sir.'

Then he made me sign a statement and let me go.

Then I was taken to the Palace of Justice, into the chambers of a judge.

The judge asked me:

'Were you the friend of the deceased Berardo Viola?'

'Yes, sir.'

'Do you agree that the deceased had recently had a serious disappointment in love?'

'Yes, sir.'

'Do you agree that the deceased was confined in the same cell as you and hanged himself from a window-bar while you were asleep?'

'Yes, sir.'

He too made me sign a statement and let me go.

At midday I was released. I was escorted to the station and put on the train to Avezzano with compulsory travelling papers. My father will tell you the rest.

By the time my son arrived at Fontamara we had learned most of what he has just been telling you from the Mystery Man.

My son arrived just at the moment when about fifteen of us were gathered round the 'stone' and the other material that the Mystery Man had given us to print the peasants' own paper – the first peasants' own paper. The 'stone' was a wooden box, with a so-called lithographic table under the lid, and acids and ink with which you could print any hand-written sheet on a white surface and reproduce any number of copies you liked.

We had placed the 'stone' on Sorcanera's table in the middle of the street, and, as I said, about fifteen of us were gathered round it, discussing what kind of paper to make.

The Hero of Porta Pia was there. He had the clearest handwriting and was to write the sheet. General Baldissera, who understood grammar and spelling, was there, too. So were Raffaele Scarpone, to whom the Mystery Man had explained the working of the stone, and Antonio Braciola, Pasquale Cipolla, Ciro Zironda, Vincenzo Scorza, Giacinto Barletta, Giovanni Testone, Anacleto the tailor, Alberto Saccone, and Michele Zompa, besides Sorcanera and me.

The first thing we discussed was the title to give the paper.

The Hero of Porta Pia wanted the kind of title they have in towns, like *The Messenger*, *The Tribune*, and so forth, but Raffaele Scarpone, who had inherited Berardo's ways, told him to shut up.

'In our paper we shan't imitate anybody,' he said. 'This is the first paper there ever has been!'

Michele Zompa proposed a good title, *Truth*, which meant a great deal.

But Scarpone wouldn't hear of it.

'Truth?' he said. 'Who the devil knows the truth?'

'We don't know it, but we do want to know it,' Michele answered.

'And when you've got it, what are you going to do with it – make soup?' asked Scarpone.

That was the way he used to argue.

General Baldissera had another good idea: *Justice*.

'You're mad,' said Scarpone. 'Hasn't justice always been against us?'

To understand what he meant you must bear in mind that for us 'justice' always meant the gendarmes. To fall into the hands of justice meant to fall into the hands of the gendarmes. To work in the cause of justice meant to be a spy, an informer of the gendarmes.

'But it's real justice I mean,' said the old cobbler, losing his patience. 'Equal justice for everybody.'

'You'll find that in Paradise,' Raffaele Scarpone said.

There was no answer to that.

Sorcanera's suggestion for the paper's title was *The Peasants' Clarion*, but nobody took any notice of her.

'What are we to do?' said Scarpone.

'We must find a good title,' said the Hero. 'You make a suggestion.'

'I've already made it: *What are we to do?*'

When, after making him repeat it three times, we realised that Scarpone's suggestion for the title of the paper really was *What are we to do?* we looked at each other in astonishment.

'But that isn't a title!' the Hero said. 'That isn't a title! What we want is a title, something to put at the top of the paper, in beautiful handwriting. Don't you understand?'

'Very well, then, write at the top of the paper in your beautiful handwriting *What are we to do??* ' said Scarpone, 'and that will be your title.'

'But it's a ridiculous title,' the Hero objected. 'If a copy of our paper gets to Rome, they'll laugh at it.'

Raffaele Scarpone lost his temper. This paper was to be the peasants' own paper, the first peasants' own paper, written by and for the peasants. What they might think in Rome was all the same to him.

Baldissera agreed with Scarpone, so his proposal was accepted.

Meanwhile the Hero reluctantly sat down and began to write out the title of the paper, while the rest discussed what the first article was to be about.

'The title of the first article must be: "They've murdered Berardo Viola." You'll all agree to that,' said Michele Zompa.

Scarpone accepted this, but wanted to make it:

'They've murdered Berardo Viola. What are we to do?'

' "What are we to do?" is in the title already,' Michele noticed.

'Once isn't enough,' Scarpone said. 'We must repeat it. If we don't repeat it, the title's useless. "What are we to do?" must be repeated in every article. *They have taken away our water. What are we to do?* Do you follow? *The priest won't bury our dead. What are we to do? They rape our women in the name of the law. What are we to do? Don Circostanza is a bastard. What are we to do?*'

Then we saw Scarpone's idea, and agreed with him.

There was a minor argument about Berardo's name. Baldissera maintained that Viola was spelled with two 'l's,' but Michele Zompa thought one was enough. But the Hero said he could write it in such a way as to leave it in doubt whether there was one 'l' or two, and that put an end to the argument.

As soon as I saw that there was nothing else to discuss I went home with my son, to be alone with him for a time, because I thought I had lost him and he had come back to me again.

It was late at night when Scarpone came to me with a parcel of about thirty copies of our paper, *What are we to do?* He wanted me to go and distribute them at San Benedetto, where I had many acquaintances. The other peasants were going to distribute the paper in other villages next day. Altogether about five hundred copies had been printed.

My wife's family lives at San Benedetto, and we decided to celebrate my son's release from prison by going to San Benedetto, all three of us. Going there was our salvation.

We left for San Benedetto on the following afternoon. I distributed the paper in half an hour. We had our supper at San Benedetto that night and started off back to Fontamara towards nine o'clock. When we were half way we heard some shots in the distance.

'Which saint's day is it today?' asked my wife, wanting to know which village the shots were coming from.

It was difficult to guess which saint's day it was. St. Louis's day was already over and St. Anne's was still to come.

'Anyone would think the shots were coming from Fontamara,' I said.

A carter from Manaforno passed at that moment, coming from the direction of our local town.

'Eh, you Fontamaresi,' he shouted, without stopping. 'There's war at Fontamara!'

We walked on.

'War? Why war?' we asked each other.

'War between the people of Fontamara? It's impossible,' we said to each other.

The Contractor making war upon the people of Fontamara? Why?

Every now and then the shooting died down, but then started again. As we got nearer it became more obvious than ever that the shooting was coming from Fontamara, and that the shots were rifle shots.

'What are to do?' we asked each other.

That was the question that Scarpone had asked. *What are we to do?*

The question was easier to ask than to answer. Meanwhile we walked on.

At the junction of the Pescina and Fontamara roads we met Pasquale Cipolla.

'Where are you going? To Fontamara? Are you mad?' he

shouted at us, and went on running towards Pescina.

We started running after Pasquale Cipolla.

'But what's happening at Fontamara?' I shouted after him. 'What's the shooting about?'

'It's war! It's war!' he answered. 'It's war against the peasants – against the paper!'

'What has happened to the others?'

'Those who could ran away. Those who could escaped,' Cipolla answered, without stopping.

'Did Scarpone escape?' my son asked.

'May his soul rest in peace,' said Cipolla, making the sign of the Cross.

'Did Venerdì Santo escape?'

'May his soul rest in peace,' said Cipolla, making the sign of the Cross.

'And Ponzio Pilato?'

'He escaped over the mountain.'

'And Michele Zompa?'

'He took the road to Ortona.'

'And General Baldissera?'

'May his soul rest in peace.'

'Who else is dead?'

At that moment we heard the clattering of hoofs coming towards us. It might have been the gendarmes from Pescina going to Fontamara.

We rushed into the fields for safety. In the darkness we lost Pasquale Cipolla. We have never heard of him since.

Nor have we ever heard of any of the others – of those who died or those who escaped, nor about our house or about the land.

Now we are here. The Mystery Man helped us get out of the country. But it is obvious that we cannot stay abroad. What are we to do?

After so much strife and anguish and tears, and wounds and blood, and hatred and despair – what are we to do?